The ROBE

Renee Christine Smith

authorHOUSE®

AuthorHouse™
1663 Liberty Drive
Bloomington, IN 47403
www.authorhouse.com
Phone: 1 (800) 839-8640

Published by AuthorHouse 02/12/2018

ISBN: 978-1-5462-2790-8 (sc)
ISBN: 978-1-5462-2789-2 (e)

Print information available on the last page.

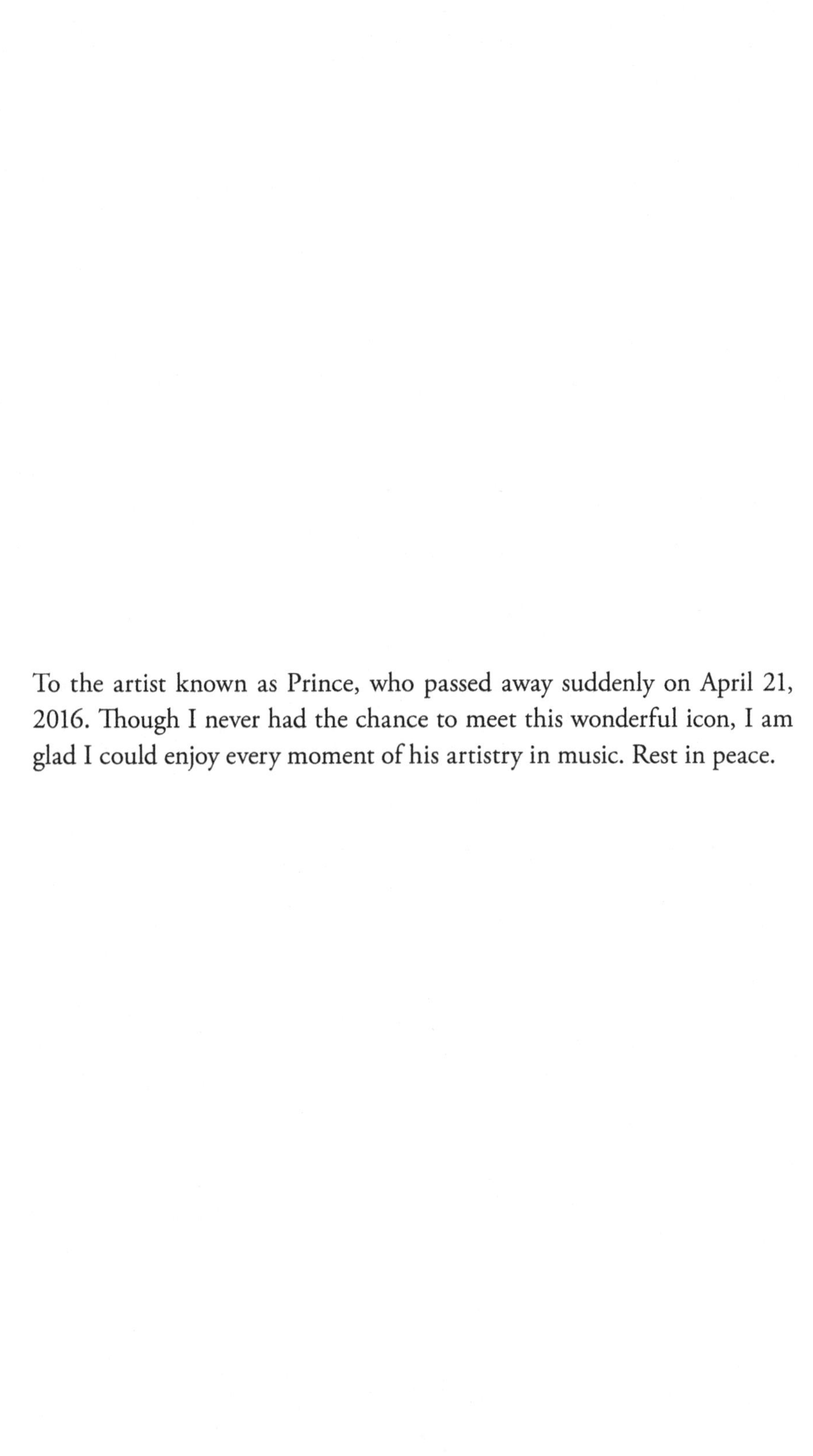

To the artist known as Prince, who passed away suddenly on April 21, 2016. Though I never had the chance to meet this wonderful icon, I am glad I could enjoy every moment of his artistry in music. Rest in peace.

Contents

Chapter 1

First Confession

IT WAS SEVENTY-THREE degrees one morning here in the small town of West Cambridge, Massachusetts, or Neighborhood Ten as it was referred to demographically. Just as I began to wake up and start with my morning yawn I hear, "Donovan Michael Mulligan! My youngest child with brown hair, brown eyes, and tiny freckles on his nose, it's time for school."

My mom, Maureen, had made herself the alarm clock for me, my brother, Timothy, and my sister, Lauren. She always woke us up in the morning with her famous greeting. There she was looking over me with her bright-red hair and loud voice. As we Mulligans began preparing for the day, it was chaos in our house. I liked opening the window the first thing in the morning for some fresh air. Sometimes, I saw a bird that looked like a cardinal on the windowsill.

"After school, you'll have an early dinner so we can go to catechism class," Mom said.

"Thank God today will be the last preparation session," I said.

"Here's a turkey and cheese sandwich with your favorites—lettuce and tomato—for lunch. There are some potato chips and a small can of grape juice, dear."

"Thanks, Mom. I'm going to catch the bus."

"Matthew, you seem anxious this morning," Mom said to Dad.

"It's just the usual Wednesday morning and getting ready for the unexpected at the twenty-third precinct," he said.

"If anyone should be anxious today, it should be Donovan. He has his class at church tonight."

"Finally, our third child will start receiving Holy Communion," said Dad.

"I've finalized the plans for the hall where we'll celebrate with family and friends after the Mass. I've ordered all the food from the caterer. Your mother-in-law, dear, will take care of the cake, and I have thank-you gifts your daughter will put together for me."

"I know I can depend on you to make it all come out just right," said Dad.

"Have a nice day at work, dear," she said.

The bell rang, which indicated that school had ended for the day. It was time to get on the school bus and go home. As usual, Mom greeted me. The aroma of food was present as soon as I entered the house.

"Whatever you're cooking smells good, Mom."

"We'll eat soon and then go to church, dear."

"I'll get my homework done before we leave, Mom."

"Good. I'll let you know when dinner's ready."

Mom liked to listen to music while she cooked. As usual, she had the radio tuned to her favorite disco station, and I heard her singing along with "Disco Duck" by Rick Dees. I came downstairs and quacked like a duck referring to the song. She laughed and began to put the food on the dining room table.

"It's time to say the grace and eat dinner," she said.

"Mom, the pork chops were delicious, and you made my favorite mashed potatoes," I said.

"It's time to leave, son. Don't forget to bring your catechism book."

"Okay, Mom."

St. Cardinal's Catholic Church in downtown Boston was built in 1930. It was designed by a Roman architect in a traditional style building with stained-glass windows depicting various angels and Eucharistic symbols. The catechism classes were held behind the wooden door next to the marble sanctuary. Beyond those doors awaited Sister Arlene, who had taught these classes for many decades. She had come from the Institute of the Blessed Virgin Mary in Arizona. As usual, she was standing at the entrance of the classroom dressed in her nun's habit.

"Good evening," I said.

"Hello, I hear you've completed your study of Catholicism's fundamental concepts."

"I have."

"Welcome! Tonight is the final class, and I'll prepare you for your meeting with the priest. First, when you enter the church, the priest will welcome you. Second, you'll need to make the sign of the cross. Third, say, 'Forgive me, Father, for I have sinned.' In later confessions, you will tell him when your last confession was. The priest will give you an appropriate penance to say."

"Our Father, who art in heaven, hallowed be thy name. Thy kingdom come. Thy will be done on earth as it is in heaven. Give us this day our daily bread, and forgive us our trespasses as we forgive those who trespass against us; and lead us not into temptation, but deliver us from evil, amen," I said.

"Very good, Donovan. That is correct. I see you've been practicing," Sister Arlene said.

For the final half hour of class, the students role-played the parts of the priest and those who were making their confessions. The teacher told the students about the importance of knowing their prayers and the Ten Commandments so they would understand God's law and what made an action sinful. She then gave us examination of conscience handouts to help us prepare for our first reconciliation.

"I'll be praying for all of you," said Sister Arlene.

Sister Arlene dismissed the class. I began walking down the hallway and saw my mother speaking with the priest. Father Carmichael was a middle-aged man in his fifties with dark-brown hair and a stocky build.

He wore glasses during Mass on Sundays when reading from the Bible. He lived in the church rectory.

"Father, it seems longer than two years since I started taking these classes," I said.

"Yes, it does seem like a long time, and today, you learned about the sacrament of penance and reconciliation."

"Father, when can I bring Donovan to the church for his first confession?" asked Mom.

"Wednesday confession will begin at three in the afternoon. I look forward to seeing both of you."

"Goodbye," I said.

The days passed by quickly, and the time came for me to make my first confession. Lauren, my sister, had big, red cheeks and freckles. She stayed after school so she could go to a chemistry club meeting. Timothy, my older brother, had brown hair and green eyes. He was at baseball practice. The one sport we both agreed on was baseball, and I couldn't wait until I started junior high so I could try out for the team. I was attending St. Peter Elementary School in West Cambridge, which is very close to Boston.

"Hey Donovan! Are you coming on the bus?" asked Kenny.

"No, I'm waiting for my mother to pick me up to take me to church."

"Good luck, and remember to tell the truth," Kenny said with a laugh.

"Funny, Kenny!"

It was raining that afternoon, but still, my mother picked me up from school in her '77 white Chevy Monte Carlo with a rusty brown interior. The funny thing about her car was that it had a license plate that read, Married to one of Boston's Finest. That referred to my dad, who was a police officer. We arrived quickly, and she parked the car in front of the church. We entered and saw many lights and candles.

"Hello, Maureen and Donovan," said Father Carmichael.

"Hello, Father Carmichael," I said.

"Father, I'll be getting my hair cut while you meet with Donovan."

"Fine. We should be finished by the time you return," he said.

After sitting down, the priest said, "Donovan, this meeting is very important in the Catholic religion. Although you are very young and it is not expected that you would have sins to confess, it allows me, the priest, to provide you with spiritual direction."

"I understand, Father."

"Donovan, I don't want you to be nervous. We'll go into the confessional booth, where we'll be sitting next to each other, but we won't be able to see each other. Before you begin your sins, you will need to say, 'Forgive me, Father, for I have sinned.'"

"In the name of the Father, and of the Son, and of the Holy Spirit, amen. Forgive me, Father, for I have sinned. Father, I want to confess that I did something very bad concerning my brother, Timothy."

"What did you do?"

"Father, Timothy gets five dollars from Dad for cutting the lawn every two weeks and puts it in his piggy bank. I have often gone into his room when he was not there and took some money without his permission."

"What do you do with the money?"

"I spend it on games at Play Jacks when I go with my cousin Kenny."

"How much do you steal?"

"A dollar each time."

"Why do you feel the need to steal from your brother?"

"Because I needed it to play video games. Dad gives me only five dollars, which I have to juggle between playing and buying a slice of pizza and a soda."

"Donovan, are you confessing this today so you'll be guided to stop stealing?"

"Father, I would like to repent my soul."

"For your penance, please recite the Hail Mary," said the priest.

"Hail Mary, full of grace, the Lord is with thee. Blessed art thou among women, and blessed is the fruit of thy womb, Jesus. Holy Mary, Mother of God, pray for us sinners now and at the hour of our death, amen."

"Now you may make an act of contrition," said the priest.

"O my God, I am heartily sorry for having offended thee, and I detest all my sins because I dread the loss of heaven and the pains of hell; but most of all because they offend thee, my God, who art all-good and deserving of all my love. I firmly resolve with the help of thy grace, to confess my sins, to do penance, and to amend life, amen," I said.

"God, the Father of mercies, through the death and resurrection of his Son has reconciled the world to himself and sent the Holy Spirit among us for the forgiveness of sins. Through the ministry of the church, may God give you pardon and peace. I absolve you from your sins, in the name of the Father, and of the Son, and of the Holy Spirit."

"Amen," I said.

"God has forgiven your sins. Go in peace."

"Thanks be to God."

I stepped outside the confessional booth and turned the corner only to hear my mother.

"How did your confession go?" she asked him.

"Ask Father Carmichael," I said.

"Maureen, I'm very proud of Donovan," said the priest.

"Bye," I said.

"It was my and God's pleasure," he responded.

The twenty-third precinct building in Boston is just a few blocks from the government buildings including the courthouse. Dad, who was six feet tall with brown hair and a mustache, was among the police officers in Boston who were considered the finest. That day, he started his shift with a morning coffee chat with his fellow police officer John Quincy, who was also Irish and had graduated with my dad from the Boston Police Academy.

"I hope you had a nice weekend, John," Officer Mulligan said.

"I did. What about you?"

"It was busy. We're getting ready for Donovan's first Holy Communion. I'm letting my wife handle all the details since she attended the catechism classes with him."

"I remember when my son had his first Holy Communion, and now he's a teenager. How time passes. See you in a bit. I'm going to use the bathroom," said Officer Quincy.

Captain Clooney, who many at the police department thought

resembled the actor Archie Bunker, oversaw the administrative duties such as reviewing correspondence, budget requests, activity reports, and interviewing and hiring civilian personnel to the department.

"Officer Mulligan, I need to speak with you and Officer Quincy."

"I'll find Quincy, and we'll go to your office, Captain."

My dad quickly found Quincy and told him about the captain's request.

"Do you know why he wants to see us?" Quincy asked.

"No, but we're about to find out."

"Captain, I found Officer Quincy," said Officer Mulligan.

"Thank you both. We've been informed that a well-known organized crime boss in the Boston community is on the FBI's most-wanted list. The Boston Police Department has been asked by the special agent in charge of the investigation to assist with some of the information he'll need to build a case against him. I also have been asked by the deputy superintendent to pick my two most notable police officers for this assignment, and I chose you two because I know you're capable of handling a confidential investigation. Starting today, both of you will report directly to Special Agent Watson."

"How long will this investigation take?" Mulligan asked.

"Depends on how long it will take to gather enough evidence to arrest him."

"Who's the target?" Quincy asked.

"Special Agent Watson will let you know," said the captain.

"I'm grateful you chose me, Captain, to work with the FBI," Mulligan said.

"Me too," Quincy said.

"Just check in with me, and keep me posted. Some days, you won't be working with Watson. On those days, you'll work your regular shifts," said the captain.

"When do we meet with him?" Mulligan asked.

"He'll contact you and arrange for a meeting. I know you and Quincy are two of our best officers and will work well together."

"Wow, Mulligan! Can you believe we'll be working on an assignment with the FBI to bring down one of Boston's most notorious mobsters?" Quincy asked.

"I guess this is our chance to become blue heroes. It's time for me to go patrol the streets of Boston with my partner, but I'll see you at the meeting," said Mulligan.

Chapter 2

First Holy Communion

THE DAY OF my first Holy Communion arrived. Everyone in the house was dressed for the occasion, and Mom was wearing the white pearls Dad had bought her for Christmas. She wore them only on special occasions.

"Donovan, it's time to leave," Mom said. "Oh look how handsome our son looks in his white communion suit."

"The white silk tie adds just the perfect touch," Dad said.

"Macy's on Washington Street in Boston had a great selection of communion suits for boys," Mom said.

We drove to the church and saw others arriving.

"Matthew, go in with Timothy and Lauren. I'll take Donovan downstairs, where the children are getting their pictures taken," Mom said.

Downstairs, they saw Sister Ellen, who said, "Hello, Maureen and Donovan. Please come over here and take a picture with the photographer." Sister Ellen told us to line up so we could begin walking upstairs. As we began to enter the church packed with family and friends, Sister Kate sang Ava Maria by Franz Schubert. I began walking toward the front of the church and looked to the right only to see my sister, Lauren pointing to me. We reached the front pews and were close to the long table covered with a white tablecloth. As the choir continued to sing, we walked up to Father Carmichael, who handed us a piece of cracker. The girls dressed in white walked up to the area where the choir sat and began to sing. I heard my name called.

"Donovan Michael Mulligan, this bread and juice represents the body of Christ. Come refresh my soul and let me never be separated from thee by sin," said Father Carmichael.

"We're so proud of you, son. Now let's go celebrate!" Dad said.

"Father Carmichael, we'll see you later at the celebration," Mom said.

"Thanks for inviting me. I do plan to stop by," he responded.

My family left the church and drove to downtown Boston. Inside the restaurant, the tables were decorated in blue, and the cake had the same design as the invitation my mom had sent out to family and friends. It read, "Join us as we celebrate the first Holy Communion of Donovan Michael Mulligan on Saturday, May 10, 1980."

There was also a gift table for guest with thank-you gift bags. As I walked around each table to say hello to my family, I heard my Uncle John, my cousin Kenny's father, telling jokes. We called him Santa Claus because he had a big, round belly and gray hair. There was no family celebration that he did not make comical.

"Congratulations, Donovan! Here are some rosaries for you. Look at this one, which is a baseball rosary," said Aunt Mary.

"Thank you, Aunt Mary."

"You're welcome. Look. It features a St. Christopher medal as the centerpiece."

"Cool!"

"Here's a Catholic children's prayer book too," she said.

"The linen on the table is so pretty," said Aunt Pauleen.

"It is," said a family friend.

"Why wasn't Jesus born in Ireland? Because he couldn't find three wise men or a virgin! So Donovan, what do you want to be when you grow up?" asked Uncle John.

"John, leave him alone. He's just a kid," said Aunt Pauleen.

"I know, but he needs to start thinking so we can determine how much money we need to give him for his graduation," said Uncle John.

"Maureen and I thank you for coming to celebrate our son Donovan's first Holy Communion," my dad said. "This is not the first time for us. Many of you remember that we had such celebrations for Timothy and Lauren. I'm happy to stand here knowing my children have been encouraged to maintain close relationships with God. Father Carmichael, would you say grace?"

"The pasta and macaroni salads are delicious. I'm not sure I'll be able to fit into this floral dress again after eating all this food," said Aunt Margaret.

"Father Carmichael, thank you again for a wonderful Mass, and please join us for lunch. The fruit platter is delicious," Mom said.

"Yes, I'll certainly have lunch, but first, I want to give Donovan this prayer card of St. Raphael as he continues to endure the journey of life. The saint will keep you safe along the way, Donovan," said Father Carmichael.

"Thank you, Father," I said.

"I'm glad to hear you say that, Donovan. And thanks for the delicious lunch. I'm going to leave so I can show up at other communion celebrations today," said Father Carmichael.

"Father, we'll see you tomorrow at Mass," Dad said.

That day was a good day for me and my family. We had only one month before school ended. We were getting ready for a trip to Ireland that summer. It was a trip Dad and Mom had been talking about since Timothy started high school. I couldn't wait to see all my relatives there.

Chapter 3

Migini's Italian Bistro

IT WAS MONDAY morning. The only one missing from my household was Dad, who had gone to work early.

"Mom, when can I start going to baseball camp?" I asked.
"Once you're ready to begin junior high."
"How come Timothy can go to baseball camp?"
"Because he's on a baseball team, and it helps him improve his pitching skills."
"I'm going over to Kenny's house."
"Just make sure you're home by lunch, Donovan."

The FBI building in Boston was at 408 Atlantic Avenue, near Seaport Boulevard. My dad and John Quincy had a meeting there.

"Gentlemen, can I get you some coffee?" asked Special Agent Watson.
"No, I'm good," both officers said.
"The time has come to tell you about the target of this operation, Vincent the Mole Mafaci. The FBI's been gathering information on him for a long time to make a case. We've received approval to implement the tactics that will help us arrest him. Vincent has the nickname the Mole because he has a distinguishing black mole on the tip of his nose. It's a birthmark his parents chose not to have removed because to them, it was a symbol from God. He's the head of the family. He has two brothers and a son who report to him," Watson said.
"I heard he's a frequent visitor at Migini's Italian Bistro," said Quincy.

"Yes he is, and that's where we'll begin monitoring him. He eats there every Monday, Wednesday, and Friday and meets with his associates then. We need to wiretap him. This is where your skills will be needed," Watson said.

"It's ironic that you mentioned that restaurant because my wife has been asking me to go there. Our anniversary is coming up, and I was planning to take her there for dinner," Mulligan said.

"The timing is perfect. We need you to go there and place a bug under his customary table. We have someone who works there as a waitress. She'll seat you and your wife at that table. When can you go?"

"This weekend," Mulligan said.

"We'll meet again on Friday to go over some details, and I'll give you the device then. Officer Quincy, you'll be in the van with other FBI agents listening and waiting for the sign that he has been able to accomplish the task," Watson said.

"When do you want to meet on Friday?" Quincy asked.

"Nine in the morning," said Special Agent Watson.

Kenny's house was only twenty minutes away in West Cambridge. That day, we had only a half day of school. We decided to go to Play Jacks to play some video games. Kenny was tall and had a slim physique.

"Hi, Aunt Pauleen," I said.

"Hi, Donovan. Your cousin is anxiously waiting for you."

"Kenny, you ready to go to Play Jacks?" I asked.

"Yes! I can't wait to play the Pac-Man video game."

"That game is always crowded," I said.

"It won't be if we leave now."

"You two be careful, and make sure you get something to eat," said Aunt Pauleen.

There were several kids in the amusement arcade. The variety of lights made the place look like a circus. George was the manager and the person we got coins from.

"Donovan and Kenny, my two loyal customers. You got an early start today," George said.

"We know how crowded it gets here, so we wanted to come early," said Kenny.

"I'm going to play Centipede," I said.

"You already know what game I'm going to play," his cousin said.

"Let's meet up noon and get some pizza, Kenny."

When our money began to dwindle, we walked to Pete's restaurant.

"Now's the time to tell you about my trick-or-treating plans," I said. "We're going to get two costumes each."

"Why two?" Kenny asked.

"We'll go around once in one costume, and then we'll go around again in another costume. Twice as much candy!"

"How are we going to convince our mothers to buy us two costumes?" asked Kenny.

"We'll ask our Grandmas to buy one of them."

"Donovan, I'll leave all the details and scheming to you. We need to get home."

I walked home and was greeted by Muffie, our green-eyed cat with black and white fur. She brushed her tail on my leg as I walked in.

"Donovan, did you have fun?" Mom asked.

"Yes, and now, I'll watch some TV," I said.

"Your father will be home shortly."

My father came home looking energetic, which was expected because he had stopped at the gym.

"How's my wonderful family? Did everyone have a nice day?" he asked.

"Yes," everyone said.

"Go freshen up because dinner will be ready in a few minutes," Mom said.

"I'll be right back," her husband said.

Dinner was good. As Lauren cleaned the table and dishes, I went up to Timothy's room. My parents stayed downstairs.

"Maureen, I'm glad we're alone. I want to talk to you about this weekend," said Dad.

"Are you referring to our anniversary?"

"Yes, and I'd like to take you to Migini's."

"I'm finally going to have dinner at one of the best Italian restaurants!"

"I'll make reservations," said Dad.

"Great. I'll find out if my mother can sit for the kids."

Saturday was my parents' anniversary. We children were going to our Grandpa Teddy and Grandma Irene's house. Mom was wearing a nice pink dress and white, sling-back shoes with tiny pink bows on the front. Dad was in a nice men's gray sports jacket and black pants.

"Matthew, I think your black shoes will look nice with your outfit," Mom said.

"I agree. Are the kids ready to leave?"

"I'll check," she answered. "Donovan, Timothy, and Lauren, are you ready leave?"

"Yes, Mom," we answered.

"Everyone get in the car," Dad said.

We left for our grandparents' house, which was in Somerville, only three miles away. The car smelled of the cigarettes my dad smoked.

"Look who it is, Teddy! Our favorite grandchildren," said Grandma Irene.

"Come give your grandpa a hug, Donovan," said Grandpa Teddy.

"Maureen, you look nice, and pink is a good color for you," said her mother.

"Thanks, Mom."

"Happy anniversary, Matthew," said his father-in-law.

"Thanks, and we'll see you later. Kids, be good," said Dad.

My folks left for the restaurant, and Grandma Irene offered us some Irish soda bread cookies she'd baked. Every time we visited there, Grandpa Teddy would tell us stories. He was a tall man who walked with a limp due to an injury he had suffered many years earlier. I wondered what story he would tell us that time.

"How about my favorite grandchildren come sit over here," said Grandpa Teddy.

"Okay," we answered.

"Even though you'll be going to Ireland soon, it's important for you all to know that my parents, Donnelly and Marlene, left a small town in Ireland called Ennis Island for an opportunity to go through the golden door, which was considered the gateway to many opportunities in America. Irish people were treated like second-class citizens, and they were denied access to jobs and in some cases housing. But all that changed in time, and we became a very important ethnic group here in America," said Grandpa Teddy.

"These cookies are delicious. Can I have some more?" I asked.

"You sure can, and here's some milk too," said Grandma Irene.

Donovan followed his grandma to the kitchen and asked her about buying a Halloween costume for him. "Grandma Irene, you know Halloween is my favorite time of the year."

"Sure, and what are you going to be this year?" she asked.

"I want to go as the clown."

"Sounds scary."

"Do you think you can buy my costume?"

"Doesn't your mom usually buy one for you?"

"She does, but with all the other things she buys for me for school, I wanted to give her a break."

"Such a sweet boy. Sure, I'll buy your costume."

"Thanks, Grandma."

Migini's was a restaurant in downtown Boston near the docks. It offered valet parking and had a red, white, and green awning that stuck out over the door and windows.

"Hello, we're the Mulligans. We have reservations for two," Dad told the hostess.

"Yes, please follow me," she said.

"How nice we can sit here and see the water and the boats," said Mom.

"This is a good place to sit."

"Can I get you two something to drink?" asked the waitress.

"Wine would be good. We're celebrating our anniversary," said Dad.

"What kind of wine would you like?"

"Red," said Dad.

"Two glasses of red coming right up."

"How about some appetizers to start, honey?" asked Mom.

"Calamari and fried ravioli with cheese sounds good."

"Here are your glasses of red wine. Are you ready to order?" asked the waitress.

"Yes. We'll start with these two appetizers," said Dad.

"Good choices. They're our most popular. What about your meals?"

"I'll have shrimp scampi with pasta," said Mom.

"I've been told to order lasagna here," said Dad.

"That's another of our popular dishes. You won't be disappointed."

"Here's a toast to my wife on our anniversary and for making me a proud husband and father every year," said Dad.

The time came for my dad to place the bug under the table.

"Matthew, I'm going to the ladies' room before dessert," said Mom.

"Okay. I'll see what's on the menu."

"Mulligan, now's the time," said Officer Quincy, who was outside, into his microphone.

"Excuse me, sir, but you dropped your napkin," said the waiter.

"I'm picking up my napkin under the table and putting the wiretap in place," Matthew whispered into his microphone.

"Good job. We can hear conversations going on around you clearly," said Officer Quincy.

"Ready for dessert, Maureen?" he asked.

"New York cheesecake is what I'd like to have," said Mom.

"May we have some coffee with our dessert?" Dad asked.

"Sure," said the waitress.

"This has been the best anniversary. Thanks for such a nice evening," said Mom.

Chapter 4

IRELAND

IRELAND, HERE COME the Mulligans! The school year had ended for all of us, and we were finally leaving to go visit our relatives. My parents had planned this vacation. Lauren, Timothy, and I would be visiting the country for the first time. It was exciting to finally go and see the place where our ancestry began.

"Officer Mulligan, I wish you a safe trip. We'll continue with the investigation when you return. I'm happy with the progress you've made so far," said Special Agent Watson.

"Thank you, and I look forward to picking up where we stopped," Mulligan said.

"Have a nice vacation," said Quincy.

"See you in two weeks," said Mulligan.

Dad left the police station and came home. I could tell by his expression that he was ready to go on vacation. He had a few things around the house that he needed to take care of such as watering the plants outside.

"Can I get some goldfish when we come back from our trip?" I asked.

"Yes," Dad said.

"Matthew, I have everything packed," said Mom.

"What about our passports?"

"In my purse. Also, my father offered to come by the house and pick up our mail. Everyone will need to go to bed early because we have to be at the airport two hours early," said Mom.

"What time is our flight?" I asked.

"Eleven."

"Thank God Dad was able to get a nonstop flight," said Lauren.

On Sunday, July 6, 1980, we were about to leave for Boston's Logan Airport. The flight to Shannon would take just under ten hours, and one of our cousins would pick us up.

"Timothy, do you have your Walkman?" Mom asked.

"Yes."

"Lauren, do you have your Nancy Drew book?"

"Right here next to my bag, Mom."

"I think we're ready to drive to the airport," said Mom.

We drove to the airport in Dad's blue Chrysler. Of course, Dad had to stop for cigarettes.

"Matthew, is it really necessary for you to stop now?" his wife asked.

"Cigarettes are too expensive at the airport."

"Okay."

We pulled into Logan International and drove to the parking lot.

"I guess I should park in the long-term section," said Dad.

"When are you returning?" asked the parking attendant.

"In two weeks," answered Dad.

"Then this is the correct parking lot. Here's your voucher."

We took the shuttle bus to the Continental Airlines terminal and had some breakfast.

"May I help you?" the cashier asked.

"These three will have pancakes. We'll have scrambled eggs and toast," said Mom.

"Anything to drink?" the cashier asked.

"Yes, two coffees and three apple juices," said Mom.

"Your total is twenty-five dollars," said the cashier.

"I see some seats over there," said Dad.

"Welcome to flight 3447. I'm your pilot, John O'Shea. Please fasten your seat belts as we prepare to take off."

"I can't smoke on the plane," said Dad.

"Just go to sleep. When you wake up, we'll hopefully be close to landing," said Mom.

"Excuse me. What would you like for lunch?" the flight attendant asked the children.

"What do you have?" I asked.

"Tuna fish sandwiches or chicken sandwiches with potato chips."

"I don't want any tuna or chicken, but can I have some potato chips?" I asked.

"Yes, and what can I get for the both of you?" the flight attendant asked Lauren and Timothy.

"Tuna fish," they both said.

"In just twenty minutes, we'll show a movie, *Saturday Night Fever*, produced by Robert Stigwood," she said.

The pilot came over the loudspeaker and announced, "Ladies and gentlemen, welcome to Ireland." We had finally arrived, and it was exciting. We walked off the plane and went to the baggage claim area. As we waited for our luggage, our cousin Anthony came to us. He resembled my dad except he had a beard. We got in his van. On the way, we saw the beautiful, green country.

"Welcome to Ireland!" Anthony said. "The family is excited to have all of you here. I like to take this route. It gives you a good view of our pretty scenery on the Emerald Isle. There's our church, Saint Columba's, which we'll attend Sunday morning for Mass. It's been in existence since 1869. Matthew, it's good to see you. Ever since you told us you and your family would be coming, we've been preparing for your visit here in Limerick."

"Please let me help you with the luggage, Anthony. Timothy, take some of our luggage," said Dad.

"Welcome, Mulligan family. Let me introduce you to your cousins. Here is Brianna, Cassidy, and Aedan, who are all my children, and this is my wife, Fiona," Anthony said.

"Fa'lite, Cousin Matthew. It's been a long time since we last saw you. We're so excited to have you here," said Fiona.

"It certainly is good to see all of you too, Cousin Fiona," said Dad.

"Donovan, give your cousin Carroll a hug," he said. "Meet my wife, Claire, and children Colleen, who is the same age as you, and my son, Brendan," he said.

"Hi, cousins," said Cousin Carroll's family.

"Cousin Matthew, I promised a good sham, or as the English say, a friend, that we would visit his home. Remember the last time you were here with Maureen, he had a party at this home?" Anthony asked.

"How could I forget? I had too much to drink that time."

"Yes, and you were acting like a flute, which means drunk," said Mom.

"Ah! So, Maureen has a Muppet's, which means a sharp, tongue," Anthony said.

On our second day at my cousin's house, we were in for a treat—Aunt Fiona cooked us what's called a full Irish breakfast, which meant bacon, sausages, black and white puddings, eggs, vegetables, and potatoes all fried in creamery butter. She even made homemade Irish soda bread too.

"Maureen, would you like some Lyon's breakfast tea?" asked Fiona.

"Tea would be fine, and a glass of orange juice," she responded.

"Are we going to see the sheep farm today?" I asked Anthony.

"Donovan, I'll take the whole family there so you can see what we do to make yarn."

"Now I understand where Mom gets the yarn she uses to knit," I said.

"Knitting is a craft here in this country. Your Aunt Fiona gives tourist knitting tours also on the farm," said Anthony.

"Lauren, do you knit like your mom?" asked Fiona.

"No, but Mom's tried to teach me."

"Brianna knows how to knit, and she helps me with the tours," said Fiona.

"I still have the cream-colored Irish sweater you knitted for me two years ago. Every time I wear it to school, I get lots of compliments," said Lauren.

"The mushrooms and tomatoes in this fry-up are delicious," said Dad.
"Thank you," said Fiona.

After breakfast, we walked to the sheep farm. I was amazed at how many there were. I started counting and stopped after thirty. Many were grazing, and more were in the barn. Cousin Anthony took us over to where the yarn was made.

"Cousin Anthony, is it true that there are leprechauns here?" I asked.

"As you may know, little one, leprechauns are key figures in Irish mythology. If you find one of the little people here on the farm, according to folklore, you may find his pot of gold."

"Look at the baby sheep," said Dad.

"Wow! They're small," said Lauren.

"This is where we have the knitting tours. It's really like a store because tourists can purchase yarn and other knitting supplies," said Brianna.

A few days later, we visited a castle called Ennis Abbey. It was a thirteenth-century building.

"How do you pronounce this word, Dad?" I asked.

"Franciscans," his brother said.

"How do you know that, Timothy?" I asked.

"Because we studied about them in history class."

"Your brother's correct," said the tour guide. "The Franciscans are a Christian religious order founded in the early thirteenth century by Saint Francis of Assisi."

"Am I looking at décor from the thirteenth century?" I asked.

"Not just the décor—other artifacts here are from the same period," said the tour guide.

"It's time to drive to Cousin Carroll's for dinner," Anthony said.

We went to Cousin Carroll's house, and as soon as we entered, we saw pictures on the wall of our family. There were many relatives including my dad and his brothers. This was our last Irish meal before we left the next day.

"Claire, you must give me the recipe for this delicious Irish stew," Mom said.

"I will. It's my grandmother's recipe," she said.

"I enjoyed this visit and would like to come again," I said.

"Donovan, you can come visit anytime. Let's get ready for Mass this evening," Anthony said.

Heavy rain continued to pour during the last two days we were there, but our trip would not have been complete without the entire Mulligan family going to Mass at St. Columba's Church.

"Hello, Father Donahue, this is my family from the United States," Anthony said.

"We are pleased to have you join us for Mass," he said.

"It's a blessing to attend your Mass service," said Dad.

Chapter 5

VINTAGE NIGHTCLUB

IT WAS FALL. The leaves had begun to turn orange and yellow, which meant my favorite day was almost there. Everyone at home seemed to be carrying out their daily responsibilities, including my dad, who continues to work long hours.

"Officer Mulligan and Officer Quincy, I am happy to meet with you. We've made significant progress with our investigation regarding the Mafaci crime family. However, there's still a lot of work we need to do. I'll tell you about the next complicated task you'll tackle," Watson said.

"We're up for the challenge, Agent," Mulligan said.

"As you know, Vincent has captains who work under him. One of them is Giuseppe Meatballs Mafaci. He's the son of Vincent. Growing up, spaghetti with plenty of meatballs was his favorite dish. His son owns Vintage, a popular nightclub. We have confirmation that a casino is under the club, and gambling is illegal here in Massachusetts," Watson said.

"Agent Watson, this must be a coincidence. My wife's been wanting to go dancing there because she is as I call her a disco bunny," Mulligan said.

"Disco is the main genre of music there. If she wants to go, here's an opportunity," Watson said.

"My wife doesn't listen to disco, so it would be much harder for me to convince her to go," Quincy said.

"We need you two to get access into the casino," Watson said.

"I'll ask my wife if she wants to go this weekend. What about you, John?"

"Since I have no choice, I'll talk to my wife too," he said.

"Good luck. Let's meet Monday morning," Watson said.

Mom picked me up from school that day because she wanted to take me to get my hair cut. How ironic—she asked me about Halloween.

"Donovan, you haven't told me what you want to be for Halloween," Mom said.

"Eddie Munster from *The Munsters*."

"Let's get your costume after your haircut."

"Sounds good, Mom."

"I need to buy some candy too for our trick-or-treaters," Mom said.

Mom took me to get my hair cut and then to the supermarket for candy. Dad pulled in the driveway and walked over to the mailbox to get the mail.

"Hi, Maureen and Donovan," Dad said.

"We're having leftovers tonight, honey," Mom said.

"I'm not hungry. I had a very late lunch today," he said.

"Donovan, go wash your hands while I heat up dinner," Mom said.

"Maureen, how would you like to go dancing this weekend?" Dad asked.

"Excuse me? Did you just say dancing?"

"Yes, dancing. Why?"

"Because I don't recall you ever indicating that you liked to dance."

"Surprise! I heard about a fun place to go dancing and thought you might want to make it a double date this weekend with John and his wife."

"A double date?"

"It'll be a chance for you to meet his wife."

"I'm in!"

The weekend arrived, and once again, my parents were going out to the Vintage nightclub, a hot spot for disco in Boston. As usual, Mom had her favorite radio station on as she was getting dressed. As she styled her short, red hair with flicks all the way around the bottom, I noticed she was wearing big loop earrings. She put a floral hairpiece on. Her jersey halter dress swung with her silver, knee-high boots. Dad surprised everyone with a silver shirt and black, bell-bottom pants. The two of them walked down the stairs singing "I Love to Love" by Tina Charles.

"Donovan, you ready for us to take you to Kenny's house?" Mom asked.

"Yes."

"Make sure you listen to your Uncle John and Aunt Pauleen," Dad said.

"I will."

"Matthew, you don't need to stop again for cigarettes, do you?" Mom asked.

"No, I should have enough to last me the evening."

"Here we are. We'll see you later," Dad said.

"Bye," I said.

Vintage had a cool sign outside, and inside were disco balls hanging from the ceiling. It had a disco party backdrop dance floor with an array of colors. There were five bars and seating lounges with small leather couches.

"Look at the long line of people wrapped around the club," Dad said.

"That's what happens when you go to the hottest club in Boston," Mom said.

"But the line seems to be moving quickly."

"Do you see John?"

"No, but we decided it would be best to meet inside," he answered.

"Good idea."

"Hey Matthew! Over here," said John.

"Hi, John and Shirleen. Meet my wife, Maureen," Dad said.

"Hi. We finally get to meet you," John said.

"Shirleen, would you like to come with me to the restroom?" Mom asked.

"It's a good idea to freshen up now," said Shirleen.

"Matthew and John, we'll be right back," said Mom.

After the women walked off, John asked, "Matt, where do you think we should start looking?"

"Let's walk around and get the layout of this club. Here come the women," said Dad.

"Ladies, what can I get you to drink?" John asked.

"A rum and Coke," Mom said.

"I'll have the same," said Dad.

"Okay. We'll get the drinks," John said.

"Ladies and gentlemen," came an announcement, "welcome to Vintage, where your disco fantasies come alive. Tonight, I am happy to tell you that Larry, our dance instructor, will teach the hustle to anyone who wants to learn it," said the disc jockey.

"Maureen, I don't know how to do the hustle, but I'd like to learn," Shirleen said.

"What are we waiting for? I hear 'The Hustle' by Van McCoy."

"John, I'm going outside for a smoke. Be back shortly," said Dad.

"I'll scope out the place," said John.

"Excuse me, but can I use your lighter?" a club member asked Dad.

"Sure. Do you know why those cars are turning inside the gate?" asked Dad.

"This must be your first time here," said the club member.

"Yes it is."

"That's the special entrance for VIP members."

"Celebrities too?"

"I heard there's a special card they're given to show at the door. It gets them into the VIP lounge area, which is usually roped off and has security standing there."

"I better go in before my wife comes looking for me," said Dad.

"Over here, Matthew. Let's dance to 'Come to Me' by France Joli. I like the décor here. Let's walk over and see it after this song is over," Mom said.

The wall was decorated like a recording studio. There were at least three long rows of colorful 45-rpm records in glass frames.

"Look at all the records on the wall," said Dad.

"Wow. There's 'Grease' by Frankie Valli, 'Shadow Dancing' by Andy Gibb, 'Love Is in the Air' by John Paul Young, and my favorite, 'Souvenirs,' by Voyage. Matthew, I had so much fun and would like to come back again. I want to dance one more time before we leave," Mom said.

"Why am I not surprised? Lead the way to the dance floor," he said.

"Look—that guy's doing the robot dance. I saw them dancing the robot this morning when I was watching the dance show *Soul Train* on TV," she said.

"John and Shirleen, we enjoyed your company here," Mom said.

"We did too. Drive safely. I'll see you at work," said John.

Chapter 6

Underground Casino

MONDAY STARTED A new week for our family. For me, it just meant it was getting closer to the day Kenny and I would grab lots of candy. Dad was continuing to stay busy at his job.

"Donovan, go see who's ringing the doorbell," Timothy said.

"Hi, Grandma," I said.

"Hi, Donovan. I wanted to give you this clown costume I found at the party store."

"Wow! It's perfect!"

"And here's some makeup the store clerk said would work with the costume."

"Thanks so much, Grandmother. I can't wait to wear this!"

"I know your mom isn't home yet, but Timothy, come give your grandmother a hug before I leave," said Grandma Irene.

"Hi," said Timothy.

"I hope you're doing your homework," she said.

"Yes. Mom has a no-watching-television rule until she gets home," said Timothy.

"Goodbye. See you all soon," she said.

"Bye, Grandma."

Once again, Dad and John were meeting with Watson in his tenth-floor office, which offered a perfect view of Boston. The office was filled with mahogany furniture and pictures on the wall showing medal ceremonies.

"Officers Mulligan and Quincy, I'm anxious to learn about your discovery at the nightclub."

"We got in, Agent Watson," Mulligan said. "I learned there's a separate entrance for VIP members. Also, downstairs on the floor where the restrooms are is another entrance, which has two security guards. While I was outside smoking, someone told me that VIP members get cards that get them in there."

"Good work. But we need to get inside and play some poker," the agent said.

"I know how to play poker," said Quincy.

"It'll be important for you know how to play various poker games including Texas Hold'em," the agent said.

"Texas Hold'em is one of my favorites," Quincy said.

"Good. Teach Mulligan the game."

"I'd like to learn it," Mulligan said.

"The next few weeks will be crucial. Expect a call from me the night you'll need to go back to the club," the agent said.

"We will."

"Matthew, come by my house on Thursday so I can show you how to play," John said.

"Thursday sounds good. Thanks."

St. Peter Elementary School was a brick building with a statue of the Blessed Mother in front. It was a traditional elementary school with several classrooms of desks and chairs. Nuns taught most of the classes.

"Hey Kenny, come over here," I said.

"Donovan, what's up?" my cousin asked.

"I got my clown costume from Grandma Irene."

"You did? I decided I'll be an Indian for my second costume since my first costume is a mask that covers my face."

"Good idea. See you on Friday," I said.

Thursday arrived, and Dad was anxious to learn how to play poker. He arrived at John's house, a brick, two-story condo where the residents park their cars on cobblestone streets.

"The easiest way for me to explain this to you is to go over some of the poker hand rankings. A royal flush is the ace, king, queen, jack, and ten all of the same suit," John said.

"It looks like the hand I'm holding. This is going to be fun to learn," said Dad.

"If you come every Thursday until Watson calls us to begin playing in the underground casino, you'll become a pro."

"Thursdays are good for me. Thanks, John."

Friday, October 31, 1980, was a day of ghost and goblins. All the homes in the neighborhood were decorated with Halloween paraphernalia. Even our house had a wicked witch surrounded by orange pumpkins on the front lawn.

"Hi, Aunt Pauleen," I said.

"Who might you be?" asked Aunt Pauleen.

"Eddie Munster," I said.

"And I'm Frankenstein," said Kenny.

"What a scary mask! Let me take a picture of both of you. Now remember the rules—be back here by eight," Mom said.

"Okay, Aunt Maureen," said Kenny.

"Here's some chocolate to start your trick or treating," Mom said.

"Thanks," we responded.

"Let's cross the street and start with the houses there," said Kenny.

The sun went down in West Cambridge. Our second costumes were in the shed at Kenny's house. We creeped past his house and went inside to change costumes.

"Trick or treat!" we said.

"You look like a colorful clown," said the person who answered the door.

"Thank you for the candy, ma'am."

"I'm an Indian," said Kenny.

"Here's some candy."

"Wow, Donovan, we racked up so much more candy," said Kenny.

"It's time to go back and change into our first costumes," I said.

"How are you going to sneak all this candy into the house?"

"Give me some comic books," I said. "When my mother asks me what's in this bag, I'll tell her comic books."

"Okay," said Kenny.

Chapter 7

Texas Hold'em

THE YEAR WAS moving fast for the Mulligan family. Changes were about to happen for everyone in our family, especially for my dad.

"Captain Clooney, you wanted to speak with me?" Officer Mulligan asked.

"Yes. I'm afraid I have some bad news. Last night, Officer Quincy was in a car accident on his way home from having dinner with his wife. He's suffered a severe leg injury and won't be able to continue the FBI investigation with you. I'm going to the hospital now. Would you like to go with me?" Clooney asked.

"Yes, I would. I'm sorry to hear this."

"Me too."

"What hospital?"

"Mass General."

"How's Shirleen?"

"Lucky for her, she wasn't injured. The car was hit on John's side."

"May I help you?" the receptionist asked them.

"We're here to see John Quincy," Mulligan said.

"He's in room 207. Here are your passes."

"Thank you," said Clooney.

The second floor of the hospital was equipped with several rooms for patients and several windows. Doctors and nurses and others on staff took care of the patients.

"John, what are you doing in that cast?" Mulligan asked.

"Hi, Captain Clooney and Matt. I wish I had a good answer, but it all happened so fast."

"We wanted to see how you were doing. If there's anything you need, please let me know. I've been in touch with personnel to let them know you'll need to take a medical leave of absence," said Clooney.

"Thanks, Captain. The doctor told me I'll need surgery and then have to go to rehab for three months. Matthew, this is a setback regarding the FBI investigation, but I know you'll be able to handle it alone."

"John, just focus on getting better," said Matthew.

"Get some rest, John. We'll be in touch with Shirleen after your surgery," the captain said.

"Thanks for stopping by," Quincy said.

"Captain, thanks for bringing me here. He's lucky it wasn't more than just his leg that was injured. Hopefully, after his surgery, his leg will be okay. I'll meet with Watson and let him know."

"I'll speak with you soon," the captain said.

It was a busy day as usual at FBI headquarters in Boston. Dad was meeting with Special Agent Watson to let him know about his partner.

"Special Agent Watson, I just came from visiting Officer Quincy at the hospital," said Officer Mulligan.

"How's he doing?"

"He'll need surgery and then rehab for a couple of months."

"I'm just glad it wasn't more serious. I'll have my secretary send him a gift basket."

"Nice," said Officer Mulligan.

"Now to change the subject back to the investigation. I'm pleased to tell you that you're making significant progress with the Mafaci investigation. The FBI has been able to get you access into the underground casino. You think you're ready to play Texas Hold'em?"

"Yes. And tomorrow, I'm going to Caesar's Palace in Atlantic City to play."

"To play or practice?" Watson asked.

"Both."

"Good. I'll get you some money to play poker with there. I'll ask you to sign for a thousand dollars for Atlantic City. If you're lucky, you won't lose it."

"A grand is more than enough. It'll give me a chance to play there for a long time, which should build up my confidence," Mulligan said.

"How did you feel after playing with Officer Quincy?"

"It felt good, but it's not the same as playing in a casino with real players and dealers."

"Good observation. Let's meet next Monday so you can let me know about your playing experience."

"I will," Matthew said.

Timothy worked at a pet shop in West Cambridge on a main street; it had parakeets and gerbils in the window. One day, Dad surprised me by picking me up from school so we could buy the goldfish he promised after we came back from Ireland.

Honk! Honk! "Donovan, over here," said Dad.

"Dad, what are you doing here?"

"Remember those goldfish you asked me about before our vacation?"

"Yeah?"

"Well, today, I'm taking you to the pet store so we can get some fish."

"Yay!"

"The store where Timothy works is only ten minutes from here."

"Yep, I know."

"Looks like we have a parking spot right in front, son."

"Hi, Dad and Donovan," said Timothy.

"Hi, son. We're here to buy some goldfish for Donovan."

"We just got some new fish in today. You'll have a nice selection to pick from."

"Wow. Look at these, Dad," I said.

"Those are too big," Dad said.

"They're Japanese koi," said Timothy.

"Where are the little goldfish?" Dad asked.

"Over here."

"There are orange, white, and even some black fish," I said.

"You need to pick a few and a small fish tank," Dad said.

"Okay. I'll get two orange, one white, and one black," I said.

"Okay, and the fish tanks are on sale," Timothy said. "I think this one will be just fine for the number you're getting."

"We need some food too," Dad said.

"I'll use my twenty percent discount," said Timothy.

"Sounds good, son."

"Be careful with this plastic bag. Make sure to fill the tank with water and release them immediately," said Timothy.

"Okay. Thanks, Timothy and Dad," I said.

Back at home, Lauren was doing her homework. Mom hadn't gotten back, but she had told my dad that she'd bring home some takeout for dinner.

"Hi, Lauren. Look what I got," I said.

"Wow! Cool fish," she replied.

"Yep, and I'm going to give them all names."

"You should probably get them out of the plastic bag," she said.

"I will," I responded.

"I think I hear Mom," said Lauren.

"Hi, everyone. Oh look! Donovan has some fish," Mom said.

"Four total," I said.

"Maureen, I need to speak with you before dinner," said Dad.

"Sure. What's up?"

"I have to work this weekend."

"If you have to, it's okay."

"Maybe you can take the kids to the movies."

"Good idea. Let's eat," she said.

Saturday, Dad left early for work. Mom was going to take us to see *Popeye*, which had been directed by Robert Altman. Dad's work involved going to Caesar's Palace, one of the exclusive hotels in Atlantic City. It sat right on the boardwalk and faced the beach. Decorated with lots of lights and slot machines, it was filled with many other attractions.

"How many chips would you like?" asked the dealer.

"A hundred dollars in five-dollar chips," Dad responded.

"Here are your chips, and good luck," said the dealer.

The card dealer shuffled and dealt. Dad began to win some hands and lose some. Finally, he became hungry and went to lunch at a steak restaurant upstairs in the hotel. He went back downstairs to play as much as he could and then called it quits. He drove home. I couldn't wait to see *Popeye*.

"Mom, can we get some popcorn at the movie?" Lauren asked.

"Yes, but let's go," Mom said.

The theater was crowded. Mom bought us popcorn and sodas. We walked inside the dark theater and found some seats in the middle aisle. Within ten minutes, the movie began. We watched the movie, and when it ended, we went home.

"I'll iron your clothes for Mass tomorrow. We're going to the ten o'clock," Mom said.

"Okay, Mom," we said.

It was Monday morning. Time to go to school. I had a science project to turn in. The project was about the stars. Dad as usual left early for work.

"Officer Mulligan, good morning," said Special Agent Watson.

"Hello. How was your weekend?" asked Officer Mulligan.

"Good. I had relatives visiting from New Hampshire."

"My trip to Atlantic City worked out really well. I got to the casino early and played until about three in the afternoon."

"Wow! You were able to last that long with just a thousand?"

"Yes. I won some and lost some, but I came back with six hundred."

"I'm impressed. Now that you feel confident enough to play, we'd like for you to go to the underground casino this weekend."

"This weekend?" asked Officer Mulligan.

"Yes. Will that be a problem?"

"No, but I just got back from Atlantic City. I don't know what I'll tell my wife this time."

"Officer Mulligan, you have an advantage because your wife likes to go dancing. Offer to take her again, and when you go, tell her that you overhead some people talking about an incident that happened at the precinct. Do you follow what I'm saying?"

"Yes, and I assume you want me to be creative with the rest."

"Correct."

"How much will I have to play with at the casino?"

"I'll give you four hundred more to add to the six hundred you have left. You can pick it up and sign for it on Friday."

"I'll see you then, Agent Watson."

Chapter 8

Salvatore Mafaci

"OFFICER MULLIGAN, HERE'S the four hundred. Good luck tomorrow. Keep an eye on Salvatore the Gorilla Mafaci, Vincent's brother. He runs the underground casino there. Here's the pass you'll need to get in. Please call me and let me know what happened," said Special Agent Watson.

"I will."

"Remember that there will be no FBI agents in the van like last time. I can't stress how careful and cautious you need to be."

"Understood."

Mom was at the hair salon getting her hair styled for the next day. She decided to go shopping also and told Lauren to ask Dad to bring home some McDonalds.

"Hey, everyone, I brought some Big Macs, cheeseburgers, and french fries," said Dad.

"Cool! A Happy Meal!" I said.

"It's for you," Dad said.

"Thanks. I can't wait to see what toy is inside."

"I bought some apple pies too," said Dad.

"Thanks, Dad," we said.

Dad asked Timothy to babysit that evening while he and my mother went back to the club. Timothy had an important math test at school, so he needed to stay home and study anyway. I smelled Mom's perfume—Opium by Yves Saint Laurent. Dad was wearing a nice black suit jacket and slacks. Mom's usual radio station was on, and I heard her singing "There but for the Grace of God" by Machine.

"Lauren there are some ice pops in the refrigerator," Mom said.

"Okay, Mom."

"Look, Matthew. The line's not that long," said his wife.

"Good. We may be a little too early."

"Early? It's ten thirty!"

"Like I said, too early."

"We can get a drink. How's John?" she asked.

"He's slowly getting used to his daily routine since the accident."

"I understand."

"I'll get us some drinks," said Dad.

"Matthew what took you so long?" his wife asked him.

"I just overheard some people sitting at the bar talking about someone going into the precinct and start shooting."

"What?"

"I have to go there and make sure everything's okay."

"I guess I'll be okay. I'll stay over here until you come back. Be safe, Matthew."

"I will."

The separate entrance to the underground casino had tinted doors with two big *V*s printed on them that stood for Vintage. Once the doors open, a tall, muscular guy with black hair and dark eyes took Dad's special pass.

"Sir, are you going to play?" asked the dealer.

"Yes. I'd like to buy ten chips," said Dad.

"Ten chips will be a hundred dollars."

"Hey, Joe. I'm just coming around to see how things are going here at the table this evening," Salvatore said.

"Good. Just about to get started with a new game," Joe said.

Dad lost three hands but won the fourth. He was happy that he'd broken even. He decided it was time to go back inside the club to find Mom.

"Matthew, is everything okay?" she asked.

"Yes, it was a disgruntled person who'd gotten a ticket for speeding and his driver's license had been revoked. He was angry with the police officer who gave him the ticket and came to the station for revenge. Luckily, someone noticed him immediately from his court appearance, and he was taken into custody."

"Thank God! Let's go dance."

On Monday morning, everyone was out of the house.

"Special Agent Watson, I made a lot of observations at the casino," said Officer Mulligan. "Salvatore came over to the table where I was playing."

"Did anything unusual happen?" Watson asked.

"Yes. First, he walked around to all the poker tables and spoke with the dealers. Then he went into an office around the side of the bar and made some calls. Giuseppe, his brother, came in and chatted with him for a while. The money that was made at the poker tables was taken to the back, past his office. Players aren't allowed past his door."

"Interesting. Good observations, Officer Mulligan. I'm pleased to hear this. Now that we have that information, we'll take over. We'll let you know when we make an arrest."

"Thank you, Agent. I look forward to your call."

"I'll let Captain Clooney know that your assistance in this operation was very helpful and that you've done what I call a job well done."

Chapter 9

Blue Hero

"OFFICER MULLIGAN, IT'S been a year the FBI has been working this case. I can finally tell you that at three thirty this afternoon, our suspect was arrested along with the bosses who served under him," said Special Agent Watson.

"The day's finally come when the Mafaci crime family will be dissolved," said Officer Mulligan.

"Anytime you arrest the hand that feeds the organization, that creates a breakdown in the organization's structure. I commend you on getting that bug planted at Migini's that let us monitor his meetings."

"I think that part was due to my wife's eagerness to go there for our anniversary. That made it easy for me to not raise any suspicion."

"I also commend you for locating the underground casino there."

"Officer Quincy did a good job teaching me how to play Texas Hold'em."

"It's time to prepare for trial. I hope the jury will find them all guilty," said Special Agent Watson.

"Dad, you're home early," I said.

"I have good news. I'm glad everyone's here. I just learned from Captain Clooney that I'll be receiving the Blue Hero award from the police association for my role in the arrest of the Mafaci crime family," said Dad.

"Congratulations, Dad! That's terrific. When will you get the award?" Timothy asked.

"Friday at the Grandiose Banquet Hall in downtown Boston," said Dad.

Everyone in the house was excited because Dad was receiving an award that day. For his special occasion, he wore a gray suit with a turquoise-blue tie.

"Maureen, do you have your camera?" asked Dad.

"Yes I do. And we're not going to stop for cigarettes."

"Let's all go," said Dad.

Grandiose Banquet Hall was the luxury venue in downtown Boston. It regularly hosted weddings and ceremonies. Several of its banquet rooms could hold over a hundred and fifty guests. The purple carpet with diamond designs gave the spiral staircases on both sides an elegant look.

"Welcome to our guest of honor. This must be the rest of the Mulligan family," Captain Clooney said.

"Yes, Captain. This is my wife, Maureen, sons Timothy and Donovan, and daughter Lauren," said Dad.

"It's a pleasure to meet all of you. We're so excited for your father, and I'm sure all of you are too," the captain said. "Matthew, you'll sit on the stage with the guest. We have a table for your family," said Captain Clooney.

Dad sat at the guest table on the stage. The tables were decorated with nice flowers and place settings. In between the tables was a podium with a microphone. Behind the tables hung a huge banner that read Boston Police Association.

"It gives me great pleasure to introduce to you the mayor of Boston," said Captain Clooney.

"Thank you, Captain," the mayor said. "I'm honored to speak about Officer Matthew Mulligan. He has consistently shown this police department and the citizens of Boston that he cares. Captain Clooney told me that careful consideration went into who was chosen from the department to help the FBI in the investigation. Officer Mulligan demonstrated leadership, and most important, he got the job done.

"Because of Officer Mulligan, one of Boston's most notorious mob bosses, Vincent the Mole Mafaci, is going to prison for a long time. Boston no longer has to worry about Vincent and his crime family members wreaking havoc on our city or citizens. For those reasons, Officer Mulligan, I'm proud on behalf of the City of Boston to give you the Blue Hero Award."

"Thank you, Mayor. I thank the City of Boston and the Boston Police Association for this prestigious award. It was a task that couldn't have been successful without team members. I accept this award on behalf of all those who were involved. At times when things appeared to be uncertain, I remembered what Father Carmichael told me—you never fear the enemy. You make the enemy fear you. Thanks, Father Carmichael, for those words of encouragement.

"I'm happy you all got to meet my family—my wife, Maureen, and children Timothy, Lauren, and Donovan. Thanks to my in-laws and brothers Officer Joseph, Officer John, and my sister Kathleen. It makes me proud to stand here and receive this award as one of Boston's finest. Thank you," said Dad.

"Matthew, you've had a good night. Let's see what tomorrow brings," Mom said.

Chapter 10

Happy Birthday

"IT'S SATURDAY, A special day because it's Donovan's birthday," said Mom.

Matthew, Maureen, Timothy, and Lauren sang, "Happy birthday to you, happy birthday to you, happy birthday to Donovan, happy birthday to you."

"Make a wish, son and blow out the candles," said Dad.

"Wow! Tickets to the Prince concert at the Centrum Convention Center. Thanks, Mom and Dad. This is the best gift ever!" I said.

"Your brother and sister are going too. I decided to make it a family affair," said Dad.

"What about Mom?" I asked.

"Donovan, I'm not into Prince. You go and have fun, son," Mom said.

"I can't believe after so many years, I'm finally going to see Prince in concert. I can't wait to tell all my friends at school on Monday," I said.

At school, I had finished lunch and was walking to class.

"Donovan, did you know the school's having a career fair today in the gym?" asked Kenny.

"No, I didn't know that. Who'll be there?" I asked.

"People from different colleges. They want to speak with us about the future. I already know I want to become a fireman," said Kenny.

"Will anyone from the fire department be there?"

"Yes, and from the police, army, navy, and marines. Oh yeah, and the FBI."

"Today, class, for social studies, we're going to the college fair in the gym," said the teacher. "It'll be an opportunity for you to speak with professionals in many professions. Let's go. You're welcome to walk around and talk to the college representatives. I'll meet you here at two thirty."

"Excuse me, but are you the representative from the FBI?" I asked.

"Yes, I'm Special Agent Johnson."

"My name's Donovan."

"Hello, Donovan. I'm glad you came over to inquire about the FBI. That stands for the Federal Bureau of Investigation. We investigate crimes around the world and capture criminals engaged in those crimes."

"What do you have to do to become an FBI agent?"

"Donovan, there are several criteria you must meet to be considered a candidate for the FBI. First, you have to go to college and graduate with a four-year degree. The FBI sends representatives to high schools so agents can talk to teenagers who are interested in applying for the FBI training program. It's important that you don't get into trouble that would give you a police record. That's a big minus."

"What type of college degree will I need?"

"Most candidates study criminal justice in college."

"My dad studied criminal justice in college. He's a police officer."

"And you'll need at least three years' experience in law enforcement."

"Do you mean like working at the police department?"

"Yes. And the FBI requires references. We'll do background checks on your references. If you apply to the FBI, you'll want to make sure that your references will commend you as someone they have worked with," said Special Agent Johnson.

"Wow. That's a lot of stuff," I said.

"How are you doing in school?"

"I maintain a B plus in all my classes."

"How old are you, Donovan?"

"Thirteen."

"Good. You'll have enough time to prepare if this is something you're serious about. Here's some information about the FBI and my business card if you have any questions."

"Thanks, Special Agent Johnson. I'll read this."

"You're welcome. Thanks for stopping by to learn about the FBI."

We Mulligans were excited about going to the Prince concert that evening.

"Hope you all have fun at the concert," Mom said.

"Mom, what will you do tonight?" I asked.

"Some of my friends are getting together to have a knitting party," she said. "We're going to eat, drink, and laugh as we knit."

"What are you knitting?" I asked.

"A hat for your cousin Kelly. She's expecting her first baby. In this family, we always knit a special baby hat for newborns," Mom said.

"I didn't know that. Did someone knit me a hat when I was born?" I asked.

"Yes. Aunt Mary knitted you the cutest baby hat and outfit to match," Mom said.

Since this is called the Purple Rain concert, we're all wearing purple. Dad has a purple baseball cap, Timothy's wearing a purple T-shirt, Lauren is wearing purple jeans, and I'm wearing a purple bandanna. I guess you can say we're one purple-crazy family.

"I want to take a picture of everyone dressed in purple," Mom said.

"And I want us to go have dinner at Burger Irger before the concert," said Dad.

We arrived at the restaurant filled with small tables and chairs. The windows had curtains with vintage signs from the 1950s on the wall.

"What can I get for the Mulligans?" asked Jimmy.

"Hi, Jimmy. We'll all have the Burger Irger special with onion rings," said Dad.

"Coming right up. What about drinks?"

"Four vanilla shakes!" said Dad.

Dad told us, "I hope the three of you know how proud I am that you're doing so well in school and sports. Timothy, you're a great team player on the baseball team. It makes me proud to be your dad and watch you as you continue to leap toward your goals in life. Always know that as your dad, I will have your backs! And let's eat."

"Here we are at the Centrum Arena," said Lauren.

"Fans are pouring in just as excited as we are," said Timothy.

"I see you have four tickets," said the ticket agent. "Hey, don't I know you? Mulligan, right?"

"Yes, Officer Mulligan."

"Ahh, if you'd worked the concert, you could have gotten all your children in for free."

"Maybe next time," said Dad.

"Enjoy the show," the ticket agent said.

"These are great seats, Dad, here in the first section and first row," I said.

"You can feel the energy here," said Lauren.

"I think the concert's about to start. The lights are starting to dim," said Dad.

"Look all those purple lights! And here comes Prince on a motorcycle," I said.

"What a way to end the concert by singing one of my favorite songs, 'Purple Rain'," said Dad.

"That was the best concert ever, Dad. Thanks for taking us," I said.

"I'm going to stop at Benny's Bodega for some cigarettes on the way home," said Dad.

Benny Bodega was a small, neighborhood grocery store. Dad chose to stop there since it was on the way home.

"I'll be right back," said Dad.

"Why does Dad need to smoke?" I asked.

"Mom told me it's because it calms his nerves as a police officer," said Lauren.

"That was such a good concert. I can't wait to tell my friends at school," I said.

"Why are those two men in jeans and hooded sweatshirts walking toward the car?" asked Lauren.

"Donovan, is your door locked?" Timothy asked.

"Yes. Why's he banging on the window?" I asked.

"The other guy's coming around to my side, Timothy," said Lauren.

"Roll down the window," said the guy next to Donovan's window.

"Timothy, he's pulling on the handle to open the door!" said Lauren.

"Donovan, ignore him," said Timothy.

"Hey! Get away from the car now!" said Dad, who had just walked up.

The guy next to my window turned around, and before he could reach in his pocket, my father fired two shots. One hit him in the stomach, and the other hit him in the knee. He fell to the ground and started screaming.

"Dad! Be careful! There's another guy," said Lauren.

My father walked around the car to Lauren's side. The other guy, who had ducked down, stood and shot my dad point blank in the face.

"Dad! Dad!" yelled Timothy.

"Look at all the blood pouring from his face!" Lauren yelled.

"We need to recite Psalm 23," Timothy said.

"Right now?" I asked.

"Yes, now! The Lord is my shepherd; I shall not want. He maketh me to lie down in green pastures; he leadeth me beside the still waters," said Timothy.

"He restoreth my soul; he leadeth me in the paths of righteousness for his name's sake," said Lauren.

"Yea, though I walk through the valley of the shadow of death, I will fear no evil, for thou art with me; thy rod and they staff they comfort me," I said.

"Thou prepares a table before me in the presence of mine enemies: thou anointest my head with oil; my cup runneth over," said Timothy.

"Surely goodness and mercy shall follow me all of the days of my life," said Lauren.

"Amen," said Timothy, Lauren, and I.

"I'm sorry, but your father is dead," said an ambulance attendant.

"You need to call the time," said another.

"It's eleven fifty."

"I'm sorry for your loss. You all appear to be in shock. I'd like you to come with us in the ambulance so we can have you checked out," an attendant said.

"Teddy, I hear the doorbell ringing again," said Grandma Irene.

"Hello. I'm here to see Maureen and the children," said the mayor of Boston.

"It's nice of you to stop by. They're in the living room," said Grandpa Teddy.

"Maureen, my wife and I want to offer our condolences to you on the death of Matthew. We are saddened and shocked about this senseless act. I promise to make sure everything is done properly so you and your family can receive justice for Matthew's murder," the mayor said.

"Thank you, Mayor," Mom said.

"Maureen, Timothy, Lauren, and Donovan, I can't tell you how sorry I am to learn of the tragic death of your beloved husband and father," Father Carmichael said. "I've come to offer your family a special prayer in Romans 5:21: 'That as sin hath reigned unto death, even so might grace reign through righteousness unto eternal life by Jesus Christ our Lord, amen.'"

"Is Dad in heaven, Father Carmichael?" I asked.

"Yes, Donovan. Your dad is now being welcomed into the house of the Lord."

"Father Carmichael, thank you for coming and sharing that scripture with my family during our time of sadness. I would like to speak with you privately. Timothy, Donovan, Lauren, please go out of the den and close the door," Mom said.

Mom and Father Carmichael were in the den for twenty minutes. The door opened, and out they walked. For some reason, my mom had stopped crying and looked as if she were at peace with what had happened to my father. She began to talk with family and friends and even laugh. The night ended, and she was finally ready to accept the fact that we'd have to bury my father.

Family and friends dressed in black filled the church. Hundreds of police officers from around the country attended. Service programs were handed out as people went to their seats.

"Excuse me, Donovan, but it's time for the pallbearers to take your dad's coffin into the church," said Father Carmichael.

"Just one moment, Father. I want to place this purple bandanna I wore to the Purple Rain concert across my father's forehead. I want him to know that though this isn't how I wanted it to end for us, I'll always be grateful to him for taking me to see Prince. I realize more than ever how blessed I was to have him as my hero," I said.

"Certainly, Donovan. Now, you can go inside and sit with your family," the priest said.

"Matthew Mulligan was a man of great faith. He chose his paths carefully and wisely. He adored his wife, Maureen, and their three children—Timothy, Lauren, and Donovan. I had the honor to baptize and conduct their first Holy Communions. Matthew was a devout Catholic. He'd often come by the church and speak with me about life. He was very committed to his profession as a Boston police officer. He used to say to me, 'Father Carmichael, I guess I really am one of Boston's finest,'" said Father Carmichael.

"Timothy, how proud Dad would have been to hear those things about him," I said.

"The service is over. It's time to go out and watch the police officers from around the country salute Dad farewell," said Timothy.

"Look at the helicopters!" I said.

"The trumpet will begin to play 'Taps,' which is played at police funerals," said Kenny.

"Mrs. Mulligan, now that the police officers have placed Matthew's casket in the funeral car, we would like you to have this American flag," said a police officer.

"Thank you," she responded.

"It's time to get into the funeral cars. They will follow the police officers on motorcycle who will lead the procession to the cemetery," said the limo driver.

"I guess this will be the final resting place for Dad," I said.

"Yes, it will be," said Lauren.

"Matthew, who left this earth marked with the sign of faith, has entered the welcoming company of those who need faith no longer but see God face to face. Let the incense serve as a symbol of our prayers that the soul of Matthew will rise to God as the incense rises in the name of the Father, the Son, and the Holy Spirit, amen," said Father Carmichael.

My mother was full of grief. My dad's two brothers, Uncle John and Uncle Joseph, looked sad and exhausted. We left the burial site and went to a restaurant for a meal with family and friends. There, I overheard my mom talking to my two uncles about my dad.

"I'm upset that Matthew's gold wedding ring and gold claddagh ring are missing. I was told by Captain Clooney that they must have been stolen during the shooting. Those rings have special meanings because I gave Matthew that ring when we got married, and your parents gave him the claddagh ring when he graduated from the police academy. It just breaks my heart that those two men stole those rings," Mom said.

"Don't worry, Maureen. We'll look into it for you," Uncle John said.

"Thanks. I'll appreciate anything you can do to find those rings," Mom said.

"Hey, Timothy, come over here. I overheard Mom telling Uncle John and Uncle Joseph that the guys who killed Dad stole his wedding ring and claddagh ring. Hey, Timothy, do you want to be a police officer like Dad?" I asked.

"No, but it's not because of what happened to Dad. It's just that I want to be an accountant. We talked about that, and he supported me," he answered.

Chapter 11

One Year Later

THE MUNICIPAL COURTHOUSE in downtown Boston was on the sixth floor. Inside the courtroom were mahogany rows of seating. An American flag stood behind where the judge sat in a large leather chair. A court reporter sat to the right of the judge.

"Donovan, I would like you to speak to the court on behalf of our family at the sentencing," Mom said.

"Me? Why, Mom?"

"Donovan, I think the jury will have more sympathy if they heard a statement from one of the children."

"Okay, Mom."

"It's time to address the court," Judge Walker said. "We'll start with a victim impact statement from Donovan Mulligan."

On behalf of the Mulligan family, I speak to the court about why my family and I feel these two defendants should get life in prison without parole. Matthew Mulligan was not just a devoted husband and father. He was also a blue hero. He woke up every morning excited about going to work as a police officer. He made sure each day and each shift that he was doing his job to protect and serve the citizens of Boston.

But those days were cut short by the senseless act of these two defendants, or in street terms, thugs. I read a newspaper article about this case. The editor stated that the only reason these two men were having such a hard time was because one was African-American and the other was Hispanic. I'm here to tell you that this case has nothing to do with race. It doesn't matter whether these two men were green or blue. The bottom line is that they decided to live off the backs of innocent people, and they chose to do so by robbing. Juan Santiago stole my father's wedding ring, which my mom had given him when they were married, and his claddagh ring, which my grandparents gave him when he graduated from the police academy.

Unfortunately, my dad, Matthew Mulligan, was one of those people these two attacked. At one point, I thought about studying medicine when I graduated high school because it would allow me to save lives. But after this tragic event with my father, I've decided to go into law enforcement so I can keep criminals like you two off the street. There's nothing these two defendants could say to my family that would change the way we feel. These two men don't comprehend the meaning of the word *sorry.* But if you find both men guilty, they will have all their lives to sit in a prison cell and think about the meaning of the words *I'm sorry.*

"Thank you, Donovan, You may have a seat," the judge said.

"Hi, Father. Excuse me," I said.

"It's okay to cry, Donovan," said Father Carmichael.

"The moment I went up to the front of the courtroom to speak, that brought back a lot of terrible memories of that awful day. Thank you for coming, Father. I appreciate it," I said.

"Sure, but your mom told me that the two men who killed your father were going to be sentenced today. I think you should go back into the courtroom because it looks like the judge has made a decision," said Father Carmichael.

"First, let me say that this is not the first time I've had to make a decision based on the killing of a police officer," the judge said. "But you two men have demonstrated to the court that you have no remorse for killing the innocent. The fact that you tried to rob the Mulligan family with the intent to harm them if necessary is despicable. I don't know of any way to describe my regret that the two of you have wasted taxpayer money because of your unjust acts.

"After reviewing the evidence and thinking carefully, I have decided that you, Juan Santiago, who pulled the trigger that killed Officer Mulligan, be sentenced to life in prison without parole. Antwon Stevens, who assisted in this terrible crime, is sentenced to twenty-five years in prison with the eligibility of parole. Bailiffs, you can take these two men out of the courtroom," the judge said.

"Cop killer!" some police officers yelled.

"I'm so glad the judge sentenced them. Excuse me for crying, but I feel a sense of relief now that I know the two men who killed my husband will be behind bars for a long time," Mom said. "Thank you, Mary, Magdalene, and Margaret, for coming to support me and the children. We're going for some lunch down the street."

The family left the courthouse and walked down the street to have lunch at a small cafe.

"You were excellent, Donovan. Your father would have been proud. I know he's watching over us saying, 'That's my boy!'" Uncle Joseph said.

"I agree. At least we know the two of them are on their way to Kingston Correctional Facility," I said.

Chapter 12

St. Patrick's Day

"HAPPY SAINT PATRICK'S Day, or as the Irish call it, La'Fhe'ile Pa'draig. Donovan, Timothy, and Lauren, here are some shamrock-shaped hats," Mom said.

"Good! It'll match the shamrock I painted on my face," Lauren said.
"Why don't you paint one on your big mouth too?" I asked jokingly.
"Funny, Donovan," Lauren said.
"Donovan, be nice to your sister. We'll go to Saint Cardinal's Catholic Church for Mass with Father Carmichael. Then, we'll go to downtown Boston to meet Aunt Magdalene. Aunt Mary is home preparing the food for all of us later when the parade is over. Are we ready?" Mom asked.
"Yes, Mom," said Donovan, Lauren, and Timothy.
"Good. Let's go. Remember, we stay together at the parade. No disappearing acts, Donovan," Mom said.
"Okay, Mom," said Donovan, Lauren, and Timothy.

We entered the church, which was crowded. Most of the people were wearing attire that represented Saint Patrick's Day. Even Father Carmichael had a white robe with Celtic green colors because he was Irish.

"Good morning, Mulligan family," said Father Carmichael.
"Good morning, Father Carmichael," Mom said.
"It's good to see all of you on Saint Patrick's Day," the priest said.
"Yes, Father. We're going to the parade in downtown Boston," Mom said.

"Your sister Mary invited me to her house later for some festivities," he said.

"Good! Then we'll see you later, Father," Mom said.

"Enjoy the parade," he said.

"Mom, I see some parking spaces over there in the north parking lot. Wow! Look at all the green floats. The big Irish shamrock float with little leprechauns dancing around is cute. I heard there'll be Celtic dancers here today too," I said.

"Happy Saint Patty's Day, everyone. Come give your aunt a hug, Lauren. I like the shamrock on your face," said Aunt Magdalene.

"Thanks, Aunt Magdalene," said Lauren.

"Where's the rest of the family?" Mom asked.

"I went to Mass this morning, so I left early. They'll meet us here," Aunt Magdalene said.

"We went to Mass this morning too. We didn't see you," Mom said.

"It was so crowded that I decided to sit upstairs," said Aunt Magdalene.

We walked with Aunt Magdalene to the area on West Broadway that would offer a good view of the parade. The trumpet players began playing the famous Irish song "Wearing of the Green." One by one, the participants began to march. Finally came the men and women of the twenty-third precinct, where my dad used to work. Uncle John and Uncle Joseph were in the group. They waved to us, and we waved back. Aunt Magdalene left us for a moment to find a bathroom. The parade continued, and finally, we saw Grandpa Teddy.

"Hello! Happy Saint Patrick's Day to my favorite daughters and grandchildren. Speaking of daughters, I know Mary is at her house cooking, but where's Magdalene and her family?" Grandpa Teddy asked.

"Magdalene is here, Dad, but the family hasn't arrived yet," Mom said.

"You have that look on your face, Maureen, like something's wrong," Grandpa Teddy said.

"I don't know, Dad. It just seems that Magdalene was acting strangely this morning."

"Where is she?" he asked.

"She said she had to find a restroom, but that was thirty minutes ago."

"I'll go look for her," said Grandpa Teddy.

"Happy Saint Patrick's Day, Flanagan," said Mike.

"Hey, Mike! Good to see you on this joyous day. These pastries smell delicious," Grandpa Teddy said.

"Good to see you too. How have you been?"

"I've been great since I retired," Grandpa Teddy said.

"Good. I'm glad you still visit downtown Boston," said Mike.

"Yes. I see my daughter Magdalene with the red ponytail over there talking to a blond man wearing a green T-shirt. Excuse me," said Grandpa Teddy.

"Magdalene, this isn't going to work anymore," said Ethan.

"What do you mean it's not going to work?" Magdalene asked.

"I can't be involved with a married woman," Ethan said.

"Dad!" Magdalene exclaimed.

"Magdalene, who is this guy?" Grandpa Teddy asked.

"Excuse me, sir, but we're having a private conversation," Ethan said.

"I won't excuse you. I'm her father, Teddy Flanagan. I won't allow you to point your finger in my daughter's face again."

"I'm sorry. I didn't know you were her father," Ethan said.

"Dad, please. I can handle this," Magdalene said.

"You think I'm going to leave you here with this guy?" Grandpa Teddy asked.

"I'm going, Magdalene. It's obvious we can't finish our conversation," said Ethan.

"No, wait! Please don't go," Magdalene said.

"Magdalene, what's going on here?" Grandpa Teddy asked.

"Dad, please stay out of it."

"Stay out of it? I come looking for you and find some stranger pointing his finger in your face and yelling at you? Where are Kevin and the kids?"

"They should be at the parade."

"You should be looking for them. I'll see you at Mary's house," said Grandpa Teddy.

"Hey Flanagan! Everything okay?" asked Mike.

"Yes, just a little problem that needed fixing. Good to see you again," Grandpa Teddy said.

"You too. Goodbye," said Mike.

"Hey Dad, did you find Magdalene?" asked Mom.

"Yes I did. I'll talk to you about it later. I'm going to walk around and say hello to old friends from the precinct. I'll see you all at Mary's house."

The Saint Patrick's Day parade ended, and we drove to Aunt Mary's house in the suburbs outside Boston.

"Happy Saint Patrick's Day, Aunt Mary," I said.

"How was the parade?"

"Awesome! There were a lot of good floats this year," I said.

"Look who's here—Kelly and little Ellen. Where's your husband?" Aunt Mary asked.

"He had to work the parade. He'll be here soon. How are you, Aunt Maureen?" Kelly asked.

"I'm doing good and adjusting well to all the changes since Matthew's death," said Maureen.

Happy Saint Patrick's Day. One by one, the Fitzgeralds, the Mulligans, and the Flanagans arrived. Aunt Mary cooked what we Irish call the Feast of St. Patrick. We ate Dublin coddle, corned beef and cabbage, shepherd's pie, potatoes, and Irish soda bread.

"Everything's delicious Aunt Mary," I said.

"Just wait for dessert. I have chocolate cheesecake and Irish coffee," she said.

The funny thing about Saint Patrick's Day is that the coffee never gets touched because we Irish like our alcohol. My uncle Thomas had the bar filled with Irish whiskey and beer. We were too young to drink, but our family allowed us to join in the toast with shot glasses.

"Here's to my wonderful family. May Saint Patrick bring all of you many blessings and luck!" said Grandpa Teddy.

We all held up our shot glasses and said amen. The mood at the festivities quickly changed when my Aunt Magdalene's six foot two, tall, bald husband, Kevin, who was also a police officer, stormed in the house and started yelling at her.

"Why weren't you with the children at the parade? My mother told me that you were only with them at the parade for less than an hour," Kevin said.

"I don't— Now wait just one second," said Aunt Magdalene.

"Calm down and stop screaming at my daughter!" Grandpa Teddy said. "I won't have you speak to her like that."

"We'll go outside," said Kevin.

"No, she's not going outside," said Grandpa Teddy.

"Look, please stay out of our family problems," said Kevin.

All of a sudden, all the men in the house stood up. Some were drunk. Kevin looked around and stormed out of the house.

"Do you want to talk about it?" Grandma Irene asked.

"No, Mom, I don't," Aunt Magdalene said.

"I'll drink to that!" Aunt Margaret's husband said.

The doorbell rang. It was Father Carmichael.

"Look everyone. It's Father Carmichael," Aunt Mary said.

"Hi, Father Carmichael. Why don't you tell us why this day is important? Just before you arrived, we had an incident, and apparently, some family members need to remember why this day is so important," said Grandpa Teddy.

"Sure. First, let me say happy Saint Patrick's Day," said Father Carmichael.

"Father, would you like a shot of whiskey? Just kidding," Aunt Mary's husband said.

Everyone went hysterical.

"The most important historical fact about Saint Patrick is that he grew up in a Christian family. His father was a deacon, and his grandfather was a priest," said Father Carmichael.

Everyone shouted, "Yeah!" Father Carmichael continued to tell us that at age sixteen, Saint Patrick was kidnapped by Irish raiders and taken as a slave to Gaelic, Ireland. It was there that he worked as a shepherd.

"A sheep?" said Timothy.

"No, a shepherd. During that time, he found God, who told him to flee to the coast, where a ship would be waiting to take him home. After making his way home, Patrick became a priest," said Father Carmichael.

"A priest? Ha, ha, ha!" said Timothy.

"Thanks, Father Carmichael, for the history lesson. I just wish you had come before they started drinking," Grandpa Teddy said.

"Me too," the priest said.

Father Carmichael just laughed.

"Father, please come have some food," Aunt Mary said.

Chapter 13

CHANGES

"FATHER CARMICHAEL, IT'S been five years since my father's death, but it seems like yesterday. Every year on March 28, the day he was killed, our family goes to the cemetery to visit his grave," I said.

"It's good for healing that you and your family go to Matthew's grave," the priest said.

As the years passed, it became easier for us to go. We usually spend about an hour and then drive over to his favorite restaurant, Burger Irger. The owner, Jimmy, still can't believe what happened. But it makes me feel good to have people continue to speak so highly of my dad.

"How's your mother?" Father Carmichael asked.

"She's been involved in a lot of things since my father's death. Recently, she told us that she's been dating someone who is also a widower," I said.

"Do you like the new person in your mother's life?"

"Yes. His name's Jay. His wife died of breast cancer two years ago. His son and daughter are married. His son, Jason, lives in Connecticut, and his daughter, Jennifer, lives in New York."

"How's Timothy?"

"He got married two years ago. He lives in Wortham, Massachusetts. Lauren moved to Maryland. I'm studying criminal justice at Boston College. I'll graduate in two years and apply for a job with the police department. After three years there, I'll apply to the FBI," I said.

"Donovan, I'm glad the Mulligan family has moved forward. I know that your father would have been very proud of you, Timothy, and Lauren."

"Father, I just wanted to come by the church and see how you were doing," I said.

"I'm glad you did. I'll pray for you as you embark on your journey in law enforcement."

"Goodbye, Father Carmichael, and God bless," I said.

Ring, ring. "Hello! Hey brother, what's up?" Timothy asked.

"Timothy, how are you?" I asked.

"I'm great. Just checking on my little brother."

"I'm doing good. I just left Saint Cardinal's. I visited Father Carmichael."

"How is he, Donovan?"

"He's doing well. He said he continues to pray for our family."

"I'm glad to hear all that. How's college?" Timothy asked.

"It's going well. I'm looking forward to all of you coming to my graduation."

"That sounds encouraging. I have some good news to tell you about Noreen and me. We're expecting!"

"Expecting? Congrats! Did you tell Mom?"

"Yes. She's already started knitting blankets."

"That sounds like Mom," I said.

"And we're having twins," Timothy said.

"Woo hoo! That's exciting! When will the double bundle of joy arrive?"

"In November."

"Does Lauren know?"

"Now Donovan, you know Lauren was the first person Mom called after we told her."

"I look forward to seeing you and Noreen when school is finished for the summer. I'm going to summer school, but I'll make time to visit you two in Wortham."

"Sounds like a plan, Donovan."

It was Friday. I was finished with classes for the week. I went home. Mom had left a note saying she wouldn't be home until late. She and Jay were going out to dinner. Just as I turned on the TV, the doorbell rang.

"Hey, cousin! What brings you here?" I asked.

"I came to tell you some good news," Kenny said. "I'm engaged!"

"Well, congrats! So you finally popped the question to Sherry?"

"Yep, and she said yes!"

"I'm so happy for you, Kenny. Sherry's a great person. What are the plans?"

"To get married next summer. Of course, Donovan, I want you to be my best man."

"Kenny, you know you don't even have to ask. Sure, I'll be your best man," I said.

"Good. One down and three others to ask."

"Who else will be in the wedding?" I asked.

"My brother, John Junior, and some friends."

"Let's go celebrate!" I said.

"Sounds good. Where?"

"How about Finnegan's?"

"Finnegan's it is. Since this is your celebration, I guess I should drive."

"I agree," Kenny said.

Finnegan's is a small, Irish pub in West Cambridge. Many locals hang out there. It's filled with TVs, tables, and chairs.

"Here's a toast to my cousin on getting engaged! Where's Sherry?" I asked.

"She's out celebrating with her friends. It works both ways. Donovan, we have to find you a nice, young Irish girl," said Kenny.

"I know, but I haven't met anyone yet I'd want as a girlfriend," I said.

"Don't worry, cousin. You're young and have plenty of time."

"Look—there's Cousin Nicole. Hey Nicole, what are you doing here?" I asked.

"What am I doing here? I should be asking you the same question!"

"We're celebrating Kenny's and Sherry's engagement," I said.

"Engagement? Congratulations, Kenny!" said Nicole.

"Thanks. It just happened yesterday."

"I'm so happy for you, Kenny. Where's the bride-to-be?"

"Out celebrating with her friends."

"Let's have a toast, cousins. Bartender, three shots of tequila," I said.

"Here's to our cousin Kenny on his engagement," said Nicole.

"Nicole, did Donovan ever tell you about our trick-or-treat adventure years ago?"

"No. What happened?"

"Donovan made a plan for us to be able to rack up on candy during Halloween," Kenny said.

"It all started with a telephone call to our grandmother asking her to buy us costumes," I said. "We wanted two costumes each so we could make the rounds twice. I went as Eddie Munster and later as a clown. Kenny went as the as the boogie man and later as a Indian. We cleaned up on candy that year."

"Oh how funny," Nicole said.

"But wait! That's not the entire story," said Kenny.

"Lauren found my second big bag of candy," I said. "I'd hidden it in my closet. She went there looking for computer paper, and the bag dumped over on her from a shelf. She screamed."

"Oh no!" Nicole exclaimed. "What happened?"

"Let's just say all hell broke loose," Kenny said. "Let's do another shot!"

"I think we'll need it," Nicole said.

"I came back home with my dad," I said, "and just as Kenny said, all hell broke loose. Lauren told my parents I was hiding Halloween candy. Dad yelled at me and threw *all* my candy into the garbage bag. Then he shook it so the candy would get mixed in with the garbage," I said.

"Only my cousin Donovan would do something so foolish," said Nicole.

"But wait. There's more. I got back at Lauren," I said. "The weekend after Halloween, Lauren had a dance at her school, Saint Regis Catholic High. Lauren and I weren't speaking because of the candy incident. After she left for the dance, I watched some TV and fell asleep on the couch," I said.

"How could I forget about those crazy dances at school!" said Nicole.

"When she was dancing, one boy lifted her skirt, and everyone around her began to laugh. The only problem was that one of the nuns, Sister Marie, came between them and said, 'Heavenly Father, please forgive them!' My sister was accused of acting in an ungodly manner and had to sit in the principal's office for the rest of the dance," I said.

"Wait until you hear what happened next," said Kenny.

"While I was sleeping, I heard Lauren and my father enter the house, and I ran upstairs to my bedroom. My father began telling my mother that according to Sister Marie, Lauren had acted in an ungodly manner at the dance and had had to sit out the dance in the principal's office."

"Poor Lauren," said Nicole.

"Lauren stormed upstairs, and Mom and Dad followed her to her room. Her bedroom door was wide open, and they were yelling at her. I opened my door slightly and with one eye watched the trouble she was about to get into unfold.

"When my parents were finished, they went downstairs. Lauren was in her room crying. I opened my door slowly. She saw my smile getting bigger and bigger. I began to dance and do a backstroke, and I pointed at her. She knew my chance to get her back for the candy incident had come. I was happy she'd gotten in trouble. Lauren continued to cry and slammed the door," I said.

"Donovan, that's so funny!" Nicole said.

"Catholic school has a downside. When you get into trouble no matter if it's true or not, parents always believe the nuns. Even if Lauren had been telling the truth, she didn't stand a chance in my parents' eyes, and I loved it."

We toasted, and more people who knew Kenny walked into Finnegan's. Every person he told about his engagement bought him a shot of tequila. By the time we left, Kenny was drunk.

Chapter 14

Visit to Wortham

"DONOVAN, I SPOKE with Uncle Joe about helping you get a job at the police department. He'll be here shortly to discuss how he can help you," Mom said.

"Thanks, Mom. I really need his help if I want to get into the FBI ultimately."

"That's why he wants to talk with you."

"He just pulled into the driveway. Here he comes with his sunglasses and Boston Red Sox jersey," I said.

"Good. I'll make some coffee," Mom said.

"Hello, Uncle Joe!" I said.

"Hey, it's my favorite nephew. Maureen, that coffee smells good, I'll have a cup. So Donovan, your mother tells me that you want to work in the police department."

"Yes, I want to join the FBI. I'll need at least three years of experience in a related field."

"Wow, FBI! My nephew is going after the big criminals."

"Ever since Dad was killed, I've wanted to work in law enforcement."

"He sounds just like Matthew," Mom said.

"Yes he does," said Uncle Joe. "Since I've retired from the force, I have lots of time. It would be a pleasure to write a letter of recommendation for you. How soon do you need it?"

"As soon as possible so I can submit it with my application for employment."

"I'll start working on it immediately. I wish I could stay for another cup of this delicious coffee, but your aunt is waiting to go shopping."

"Okay, Uncle Joe. I appreciate your help," I said.

"Maureen, as usual, it's been a pleasure," Uncle Joe said.

"Tell the family I said hello," Mom said.

"I will, and goodbye."

"Donovan, did you let your brother know you were going to visit him this weekend?" asked Mom.

"Yes, Mom. They're expecting me this evening. I'm packing now."

"Here's some pound cake I baked for them."

"I'm sure we'll all enjoy it, Mom."

"See you on Sunday. Drive safely."

"Okay, Mom, I will."

I was going to visit my brother and his wife. It wasn't long before I reached their street and saw their ranch-style home with two garages. Timothy was outside watering the lawn.

"Hi, little brother, how are you?" Timothy asked.

"Doing good. And you?"

"Noreen and I are getting ready for the twins. Just wait until you see what she did to their bedrooms," Timothy said.

"Donovan, you finally made it to Wortham!" Noreen said. "Your brother and I never thought we'd see this day."

"It's good to see you too, sister-in-law."

"You hungry?"

"Yes I am," I said.

"Good. Your brother plans on taking you out to dinner."

"There's a good diner just a few blocks from the house," Timothy said.

"Timothy, bring me back my favorite Reuben sandwich with french fries and of course a pickle," Noreen said.

"You got it."

"Now that's true love, brother," I said.

"I always bring her something to eat from this place, Griko's, the best diner in Wortham."

"Two?" asked the hostess.

"Yes," Timothy answered.

"What's good here, Timothy?"

"Honestly brother, everything."

"I'll have the chicken Parmesan," I said.

"You won't be disappointed," the waitress said. "And what about you, sir?"

"The BLT with french fries," Timothy said.

"Any drinks?"

"I'll have a Coke," I said.

"Me too," said Timothy.

"So Donovan, what's next for you now that you've graduated from college?"

"I want to get into the FBI, but I need to work in law enforcement for at least three years. I asked Uncle Joe for a letter of recommendation yesterday."

"Excellent. Maybe you can work at the twenty-third precinct like Dad did."

"I hope so."

"It'll be exciting to have a brother in the FBI. How's Mom doing?"

"She's doing just fine with Jay. I'm glad she's moved on. I wouldn't want her to be lonely. She's such a good human being. She deserves to have someone in her corner besides me, you, and Lauren."

"Speaking of Lauren, have you talked to her lately, Donovan?"

"Not since my graduation. My chicken is delicious! How's your job as an accountant?"

"The firm I work for in Wortham just keeps growing. It's opening branches in Chicago and Houston."

"Do you think you could be transferred to one of those locations?" I asked.

"Not right now, but you never know."

"Would you two like some dessert?" the waitress asked.

"No, but I'd like a Reuben with fries and a pickle to go," Timothy said.

"You got it, coming right up."

"Thanks for treating, big brother," I said.

"What do you have planned for Sunday?" Timothy asked.

"I'm going to the Red Sox game with Kenny."

"Later, I'll take you to good bar nearby," said Timothy.

"Timothy, it's time for me to go home. Noreen, it was good to see you again, and our family is excited about the twins," I said.

Chapter 15

Father Carmichael

THE BIG RED doors that led to the church entrance quickly became the middle aisle, where an elderly woman holding some tissues in her hand and a middle-aged man in a raincoat were waiting to go to confession.

"Welcome," said Father Carmichael.

"In the name of the Father, and of the Son, and of the Holy Spirit, amen. Forgive me, Father, for I have sinned. My last confession was a few months ago, and these are my sins. I have one sin that involves not being honest with my family about why I want to join the FBI."

"What do you mean you haven't been honest?" asked Father Carmichael.

"I feel that since my dad wasn't able to fulfill his goal of retiring as a Boston police officer, I want to step into the role to protect and serve."

"I thought your family knew why you wanted to join the FBI."

"No. I mean yes, they all know I wanted to join the FBI, but they don't know I feel obligated to because of what happened to my dad."

"Donovan, you'll have to make the choice whether you want to become an FBI agent."

"I'm applying to work at the twenty-third like my dad did. I need the experience to get into the FBI. I wanted to confess my sins so they won't be the reason why I cannot become a successful FBI agent."

"I'm glad you did. Now, you'll be able to think about how you can complete your assignments and return to the sacrament of reconciliation often. That will help you work thorough your assignment. For your penance, please recite the Glory Be."

"Glory be to the Father, and to the Son, and to the Holy Spirit, as it was in the beginning, is now, and ever shall be, world without end, amen."

"Now you may make an act of contrition."

"God, I am sorry for my sins with all my heart. In choosing to do wrong, I have sinned against you, whom I should love above all things. I firmly intend, with the help of your grace, to sin no more and avoid whatever leads me to sin," I said.

"God, the Father of mercies, through the death and resurrection of his son has reconciled the world to himself and sent the Holy Spirit among us for the forgiveness of sins. Through the ministry of the church, may God give you pardon and peace. I absolve you from your sins, in the name of the Father, and of the Son, and of the Holy Spirit."

"Amen," I said.

"God has forgiven your sins. Go in peace."

"Thanks be to God," I said.

"Hi, Donovan!"

"Hi, Mom. I just got back home too. I got a call for a job interview at the twenty-third on Monday."

"Give me a hug! I knew you'd start working there soon. When you go, make sure you wear some nice pants and a shirt with a tie."

"Okay, Mom, I will."

The twenty-third precinct building had ten floors, and inside were white floors with several desks in the lobby. The only personnel in the building were men and women dressed in blue police uniforms.

"Good morning. My name is Donovan Mulligan. I'm here to interview with Captain D'Angelo."

"I'll let Captain D'Angelo know you're here. Please have a seat," said the secretary.

"Hello, Donovan. It's nice to see you," said Captain D'Angelo. "Please come with me to my office. I understand you're looking for a job here at the twenty-third."

"Yes sir. I just graduated from Boston College with a degree in criminal justice. I plan to eventually continue my studies and apply to the FBI. As you know, I'll need three years' experience in law enforcement before that."

"Donovan, you're ambitious. I'm glad you plan to apply to the FBI."

"Thanks. I've thought about it, and based on my studies in criminal justice, I'd like to work in an evidence lab."

"An evidence lab? That's interesting. We have two officers who work in our evidence lab, and one's going on maternity leave for three months. I was planning to fill her position temporarily, but since you're interested in that work, I'd like to hire you."

"Thank you, Captain D'Angelo. That would be a good opportunity for me."

"I know you'll make a great FBI agent. I'm glad you'll be working here with us. Let me walk you to the administrative office. Marcia will help you with the paperwork. As for the salary, we can start you at twenty-eight thousand a year."

"I look forward to working here, Captain."

"I'd like you to start on Wednesday at eight in the morning. I want you to train under Officer McBride, who's going on maternity leave. You'll have a chance to see how the morning rush is for the evidence that needs processing for court cases."

"Captain D'Angelo, I'll see you on Wednesday morning."

Ring, Ring. "Hello?" asked Mom.

"Hi, Mom. I finished my interview and completed the paperwork including the drug test and finger printing. Captain D'Angelo offered me a temporary position in the evidence lab. I start on Wednesday!"

"Congratulations, Donovan! I'm so proud of you. I knew you'd make a good impression. Let's celebrate. I'll take you out to dinner at your favorite Chinese restaurant."

"Sounds good, Mom. I'll be home shortly."

Chapter 16

THREE YEARS LATER

IT HAD BEEN three years since I started working at the twenty-third in the evidence lab. The time finally arrived when I could apply to the FBI. I had the application completed and references. The only item left was my statement about why I wanted to become an agent. That would be because of the tragic death of my father.

"Donovan what are you doing?"

"Mom, I'm finishing my application for the FBI."

"Looks like you've gathered everything nicely."

"Yes, Mom. I'm going to the post office to mail this."

"I'm so proud of you for pursuing your goals."

"Thanks, Mom. Do you need anything from the store?"

"No, Donovan, but thanks."

"Okay. I'll be back later."

Chapter 17

FBI Acceptance

"DONOVAN, WHAT A surprise to see you," Father Carmichael said.

"Father, I came by to tell you I've received a letter from the FBI about my application. I came so you could pray for me when I opened it."

"Of course I will. Let me know when you're ready."

"Now more than ever, Father."

"Lord, we come before you with a special request from Donovan regarding his future in law enforcement. Whatever the outcome is, please let him be a strong man guided by your comfort and direction, amen."

I opened the letter: "Dear Mr. Mulligan: On behalf of the Federal Bureau of Investigation, I would like to inform you that you have been accepted to the Quantico Training Academy. We look forward to meeting you on September fifth."

"Congratulations, Donovan! I knew you'd been accepted even before you opened the letter."

"Thanks, Father. I feel so much better. I want to tell Mom the good news now."

"Yes, and tell your mother I said hello."

"I will, Father."

"Hi, Donovan. I was wondering where you were," Mom said.

"Mom, I'm glad you're sitting. I have some good news. I've been accepted to the FBI! Here's my acceptance letter."

"Congratulations! I'm so proud of you. I knew you'd be accepted. When do you start?"

"September fifth."

"That's only a few weeks away! You have to tell Timothy and Lauren."

Chapter 18

FBI Academy

THE DAY I'D been waiting for finally arrived. I was standing on the FBI training grounds in Quantico, Virginia. The facility was surrounded by hundreds of acres and had a state-of-the-art library, learning center, and many other facilities that made the training place unique.

"Please come in to our welcome ceremony for new trainees. May I ask your name?" the reception host asked.

"Donovan Mulligan."

"Here's your name tag, Donovan. Welcome to the FBI. Please go in and help yourself to a beverage."

"Hello. What can I get you to drink?" the bartender asked.

"A glass of wine, please."

"Excuse me. Mulligan, right?" asked Special Agent Jones.

"Yes I am."

"Donovan, I'm Special Agent Jones, the director of the training program. Welcome."

"Thank you. It's a pleasure to be here. It's been a long journey here for me. I've been waiting to be here at Quantico since I was thirteen, when I decided to work in law enforcement."

"You'll meet many other trainees who will have reasons for joining that are similar to yours."

"Yes, and I look forward to meeting them."

"Good luck, Donovan. I'm sure you'll be an asset to this program."

"Donovan Mulligan, nice to meet you. My name's Lindy McKnight."

"Lindy, it's nice to meet you."

"Where are you from?"

"Boston. And you?"

"California. Right on the coast."

"What brings you to the FBI?"

"I have two brothers who are FBI agents, so I guess you can see I had some influence."

"I come from a family of law enforcement too. My father, grandfather, and uncles were police officers."

"Ladies and gentlemen, I welcome you to the FBI Training Academy. My name is Special Agent Jones. I'm the director of the academy program. I've had the chance to converse with some of you, and I don't doubt all of you will succeed here. I can't promise it'll be easy, and some of you may consider quitting, but I promise that if you work together as a team, you'll build each other up.

"Some of the best agents in the country will be training you. If you have any questions, now's the time to ask them. I wish you the best. I'll be checking in on all of you from time to time at the training sites."

"Donovan Mulligan, right?"

"Yes I am. And you are—?"

"You probably don't remember me. I'm Dominick Porelli. My family moved from West Cambridge when I was six. But my family went to Saint Cardinal's, and you and I were in the same summer camp."

"I think I remember you."

"I remember you because my sister, Maria, had the biggest crush on you. The only thing we heard around the house all the time was, 'Donovan Mulligan is so cute!'"

"Okay, I remember Maria. She and I went through first Holy Communion together."

"Yes. Right after that, we moved to New York."

"New York. I can hear your accent. Just like some people think I have a Boston accent."

"I guess I have both," said Dominick.

"See you at training, Dominick."

The living quarters at the academy were like college dorms. The living room on the first floor had couches, chairs, and a large TV.

"You ready for tomorrow, Donovan?" Lindy asked.

"Yes. What about you?"

"I'm looking forward to getting up at five in the morning. We're watching this special on CNN about the life of an undercover agent."

"I'm going to call it a night. I have to report to training at oh six hundred," I said.

"See you in the morning, Donovan."

Chapter 19

FBI Trainees

"IT'S OH SIX hundred. All you trainees will report to the track to run a mile before you begin the defensive-driving training. At the sound of my whistle, trainees, you may begin your run," said Special Agent Dover.

Special Agent Dover blew his whistle, and there we were—trainees starting our run on the academy track. The sun was just coming up. I felt good. I'd made sure to work out at the gym in West Cambridge before I came for training. That certainly helped me keep up with the other trainees. We ran around a wooded area that led to the field. Finally, all the trainees finished. As instructed, we all walked over to the defensive driving training area.

"I'm in charge along with my associates with teaching you how to drive in vehicles as FBI agents and avoid being harmed by criminals you're trying to catch. You'll be separated into groups and assigned to one of the associates. They'll explain in detail the importance of knowing as much as you can about the vehicles you'll be using when involved in a car chase. I can't stress enough to all of you how knowing as much as you can about the car can save your lives," said Special Agent Dover.

We began to drive the vehicles between orange cones and learned several techniques used by agents engaged in pursuits. Then came the hard part—learning how to survive if you're driving at high speeds and crash. At one point, I started to learn how to drive fast without needing the brakes.

"How was the first day, Donovan?" Lindy asked.

"Good. It reminded me of my test to get my license when I was sixteen, only much faster. I'm glad to finish our first day of training."

"Trainees, now that you've had a week of defensive driving training, we're moving on to firearms. You'll learn how to safely and effectively use firearms," said Special Agent Moore.

We began to learn about firearms. I'd grown up in a house with firearms, but Dad was always careful about guns. He had a special place where he kept his firearm.

"Mulligan, when you aim for the target on the board, act as if you were in a situation where it could be you or the target. You won't have time to look around. Just shoot at the target," said Special Agent Moore.

"Yes, Special Agent Moore, I understand."

"Hey Donovan, watch this," Lindy said.

"You hit the target board right in the face! You have good aim, Lindy," I said.

"I used to go with my brothers to the shooting range and watch them. They took me only because I told them I wanted to be an FBI agent like them."

"That's good, Lindy. I didn't decide to become a FBI agent until after my father was killed off duty in 1985."

"I'm sorry, Donovan."

"It's okay. I'm proud to say my dad was one of Boston's finest."

"Good job, trainees. I think we covered enough for today," said Special Agent Moore.

I had classroom courses that started with investigative techniques and bureau operations and ended with behavioral science. The last class was interesting because the setup was like a science room. It had several newspaper articles hanging on the walls about real-life FBI cases. Those criminals were used in studies to determine what triggered the criminal mind.

It had been three months of training, and I'd learned a lot. Most important, we learned effective ways to fingerprint criminals. We'd been training a lot in Hogan Valley, which had studios created to look like real banks and stores. Actors were hired to work with us as we trained in different settings.

"Hey, Donovan, some of us are going out for drinks. You want to come?" Dominick asked.

"Sure. When?"

"In about an hour."

There wasn't much to do in Quantico. Dominick drove a Chevy Suburban, the perfect vehicle for the six of us who went to Aquia Harbor, twenty minutes from Quantico. The harbor had a pier with many bars and restaurants. It was a popular place on Saturday nights. We walked into The Dungeon, and it was crowded. We were lucky to find a little corner near one of the bars that had enough space for the six of us.

"It's been a long time since I had a drink. A cold beer sounds good," Dominick said.

"This place looks popular," Lindy said. "The first one is on us girls."

"Ladies first," I said.

"Six Bud Lights, please," Lindy said.

"Six Bud Lights coming up," the bartender said.

"Here's to all of us trainees. Hopefully, the next time we go out to drink, it'll be to celebrate our completion of the FBI academy training program," Lindy said.

"We'll drink to that," everyone else said.

"Since I'm the designated driver, I'll limit my intake," Dominick said.

"Donovan, I didn't expect you to drink much," said Lindy.

"You must be mistaken. My blood is Irish," I said.

"Oh well, say no more," said Lindy.

"I see some other trainees over there. I'm going to say hello," said Dominick.

"Donovan, do you have a girlfriend in Boston?" Lindy asked.

"No, none."

"Does that mean you're single?"

"Yep."

"People tell me I look like Marilyn Monroe."

"Really? Why's that?"

"Because I have a mole just like Marilyn did. I think Dominick's waving to you."

"This is Donovan Mulligan," said Dominick to a trainee.

"Donovan, I was your partner today in the survival skills training. You handled that critical situation in the high-risk environment we were in at the bank at Hogan's Alley," the trainee said.

"It's one in the morning," I said.

"It looks like people are starting to leave," said Dominick.

"Dominick, you okay to drive back?" I asked.

"Don't worry, Mulligan. I got this," Dominick said.

"Yee Ha! We had fun tonight," said the females in the car.

The next day, I woke up and read my emails. There were several from my mother. I didn't get any chance to talk with her until the weekends. She emailed me information about things concerning the family. The first email included pictures of Timothy and Noreen's twins—my niece Chancy and nephew Matthew.

The second email was a picture of Mom with Jay on a cruise in Hawaii. The third email was about Mom considering selling the house in West Cambridge.

I let her know I was happy that she and Jay were coming to my graduation ceremony. After I responded to all her emails, I began to search on the web for Catholic churches in the area.

Chapter 20

Special Agent Mulligan

HOGAN'S ALLEY BANK looked like most banks used every day. It was equipped with all kinds of office furniture. The inside had velvet ropes that separated the aisle for each teller's window. The first customer service desk faced the outside; across the street was The Dogwood Inn.

"Trainees, good morning. I'm pleased to announce that today is your last training course before graduation. Today, you'll show me how to handle tactical techniques in stressful scenarios during which I expect you to know how to incorporate basic tactics, investigating techniques, firearms skills, and defensive tactics that you will use to make the right decisions.

"The first trainee I'll call is Donovan Mulligan. Donovan, your first task will involve a robbery at the bank. For this task, the FBI has been asked to come and help the local police with a situation. The bank has been taken hostage by one gunman, who planned to rob the bank. You, Donovan, are there on behalf of the FBI to negotiate with the bank robber concerning his demands. My question to you is, What do you do?" Special Agent Moore asked.

"The first action I'd take is to learn the method of communication with the bank robber," I said. "It would be important for me to know what the channels of communication are so I could find out how the hostages were doing. In addition, it would help me learn the robber's name so the FBI could begin a search of this person in its database," I said.

"Very good, Donovan. How would you proceed with the bank robber once you learned his demands? Please demonstrate how you'd do this," said Special Agent Moore.

"Brad, I'm glad to hear you're willing to cooperate with the FBI. Now please let the two hostages walk out the front door," I said.

"Okay, they're both running toward the entrance," said Brad.

"Now that we have two of the hostages, I'm ready for your demands," I said.

"Agent Mulligan, I'd like to walk outside the back door with no police there and walk to my car."

"Brad, you know I can't do that when you have hostages and stolen money. If you turn yourself in now, I can keep you from being harmed by the police. But if you walk out the door and try to run, I can't promise you that things will end well," I said.

"Agent Mulligan, all my life, all I ever wanted was money. I wanted to know what it felt like to have thousands of dollars in my possession. I wanted to know what if felt like to be able to buy anything I wanted," said Brad.

"Brad, I'm sure there are many folks who feel the same way you do. But you know there are right ways to earn money, and robbing a bank isn't one of them," I said.

"Agent Mulligan, I don't think I can handle what will happen to me once I surrender, so I'll let the hostages go," said Brad.

"Good, Brad. You're starting to think about the right thing to do in this situation."

"Agent Mulligan, now that I let the hostages go, it's time for me to say goodbye."

"What do you mean goodbye?"

"Just like I said, goodbye."

"Excellent job, Donovan, in assessing the situation and the people involved and getting the bank robber to surrender the hostages. Donovan Mulligan, congratulations. You have successfully completed all tactics. Good luck to you," said Special Agent Moore.

There we were at the Quantico trainee graduation ceremony. On stage, we were fortunate to have the FBI director as the guest speaker. He stood at the podium with the seal of the Department of Justice—Federal Bureau of Investigation behind him.

"It gives me great pleasure to join the graduation ceremony for an agency that has a century of fidelity, bravery, and integrity to its credit. This day is the beginning of what some would call a special calling for you and your families. Please raise your right hand and repeat after me," said the FBI director.

"I, Donovan Mulligan, do solemnly swear that I will support and defend the Constitution of the United States against all enemies, foreign and domestic; that I will bear truth, faith, and allegiance to the same; that I take this obligation freely, without any mental reservation or purpose of evasion; and that I will well and faithfully discharge the duties of the office on which I am about to enter. So help me God," he said.

"Donovan Mulligan, this badge serves as the proof of your credentials you will take with you and use to help fight crimes. Congratulations!" said the FBI director.

"Thank you," I said.

"Mulligan, we made it!" Dominick said.

"Yes we did! What are you planning to do next?" I asked.

"I plan to go back to New York and apply to work at the FBI headquarters there."

"Gentlemen, I got a job working as a special agent overseas," said Lindy.

"I was fortunate to have been recruited by Special Agent Roth, who informed me that he tracked the progress of most trainees and decided whom he wanted to hire," I said.

"Congratulations, son," Donovan's mother said. "That was an excellent ceremony, Special Agent Mulligan."

"Mom, this is Special Agent Lindy, one of my teammates," I said.

"Lindy, how nice to meet you. Congratulations on becoming a special agent," Mom said.

"Thank you, Mrs. Mulligan. I came by to say hello and goodbye to Donovan. I guess it's fair to say, 'Until we meet again, Special Agent Mulligan,'" Lindy said.

"Please, Lindy, stand next to Donovan. I want a picture," Mom said.

"Lindy, I'm sure our paths will cross again. It's our destiny since we're FBI special agents. I'll be sure to email you from time to time," I said.

"Me too," said Lindy.

"If you don't hear from me, it'll probably be because I'm working undercover," I said.

"I understand, Donovan. How about a kiss right here on my cheek?"

"Just for asking, Lindy, you'll get a kiss and hug."

"Take care, Special Agent Mulligan," Lindy said.

"You too."

"It was nice to meet you, Mrs. Mulligan," Lindy said.

"Nice meeting you too. Good luck!" Mom said.

Chapter 21

Operation Robe

"SPECIAL AGENT MULLIGAN, we've reviewed your track record here at the FBI. Your skills demonstrate to us that you're ready for special operations," said Special Agent Roth. "You'll be working undercover to help capture criminals on our most-wanted list. We're excited that we can finally begin to get this operation underway. We feel you're the best agent to handle this undercover operation. We picked you because you have shown in your work and ethic that you can navigate your way and handle difficult assignments. The FBI has had its eyes on you, Donovan."

"I'm honored that the FBI has a special assignment for me," I said.

"Special Agent Mulligan, for many years, we've been planning how to build a case against the targets in this undercover operation. We believe you have the skills to complete the assignment. Operation Robe is an undercover assignment that involves the priesthood. Are you familiar with the priesthood?" asked Special Agent Roth.

"I am. I have a close relationship with a priest in my hometown."

"You'll be working undercover as a priest."

"A priest?"

"Yes. You'll be in clerics—the Roman collar shirt and cassock Catholic priests wear. The FBI has learned that some criminals on our most-wanted list are devout Catholics. They're criminals, but they have a need to confide their deepest and darkest secrets to others. You'll be responsible for listening and gathering information based on what these criminals tell you."

"I must say, Special Agent Roth, that I'm stunned to be given this kind of assignment. I'm a Catholic. I grew up confiding in our priest at church. Catholics go to confession. I thought that Catholics were protected by the seal of the confessional."

"The seal of the confessional applies to ordained priests only. Do you really want me to continue answering your questions?"

"No, but I can tell by the expression on your face that this is a conversation that I'd like to continue at some point especially regarding the sacrilege," I said.

"Okay, but for now, you need to know that we have specific criminals we're interested in. You need not do anything but wait for the moment when they come to you. And believe me, they'll come."

"How am I supposed to pretend to be a priest?"

"This will have to be done strategically after I share with you some important things you'll need to know concerning your assignment," said Special Agent Roth.

"Who's the target?"

"Tony Cosco. The FBI believes he's smuggling diamonds from Africa to Canada and then to the United States. That's a criminal offense—intentionally and secretively bringing items into a country without declaring them to customs officials and paying the duties or taxes. The Cosco family has been smuggling diamonds into the United States for years and selling them on the black market. The FBI has learned that Cosco's son, Carlo, lives in an independent living community in Tucson that enables adults with mental health issues to live and work in their communities in accordance with their abilities and desires. Carlo lives in the Gilmore Adult Living facility, and we believe Tony Cosco and his son are using Carlo's residence to smuggle diamonds into the United States.

"Carlo's family visits him three times a year—his birthday in the spring, Christmas, and Father's Day. Every time his family comes to visit is when the diamonds go on the black market. Special Agent Mulligan, your undercover assignment name will be Father Clearie. You'll visit Carlo and wait for him to talk to you. At some point, he will because his family's Catholic."

"What mental illness does Carlo have?" I asked.

"A form of psychosis. It's serious. But because he's not the target of this operation, we can't legally gain access to his medical files. We need you to find out the level of his psychosis so we can determine what he can and can't comprehend. This won't be an easy task, but I'm confident you'll succeed.

"We've learned that Carlo can understand certain things and does understand what his family's doing. We've been watching Carlo for a long time. He goes to the chapel at the facility. He brings a rosary and prays for a long time. He always begins with the words, 'Forgive me, Father, for I have sinned.' It's as if he wants to confess something.

"In Tucson, you'll have to speak with the priest at Saint Bonaventure Catholic Church. Father Peter has a good rapport with the staff at the facility. I'll leave the visits and plans of how to gather information to your expertise. Do you understand your assignment?"

"Yes."

"Because Father Peter lives at the church rectory, the FBI has arranged for you to live in an apartment. Here's the key. The apartment is furnished. The only thing you'll be responsible for is food. Good luck, Special Agent Mulligan. I know you'll make us proud."

Chapter 22

Father Clearie

THERE I WAS in Tucson. My apartment building was near Highway 10 and was surrounded by several golf resorts. My apartment had ten-foot ceilings, soaring, arched windows, ambient lighting, and a huge gourmet kitchen with an island and breakfast bar.

I unpacked and hung my clothes, including my clerics, in a large, walk-in closet. I decided to go to Saint Bonaventure Catholic Church to see Father Peter.

"Good morning. My name's Father Clearie. I'm here to see Father Peter."

"Good morning, Father Clearie. I'll let Father Peter know you're here," said the church secretary.

"Father Clearie, I was expecting your visit. How are you today, my brother in Christ?" asked Father Peter.

"Your brother in Christ is doing well. I wanted to introduce myself to you."

"I'm glad you did today. I'm leaving tomorrow for a conference on the Catholic clergy in Rome. The conference is for three days, and I've decided to make the visit a vacation. Father Clearie, feel free to make yourself at home here at the church. Though your stay here will be short, I'll be glad to have another priest in the church and someone who can visit the facility. I can't tell you how important our presence is for those residents."

"Yes, Father, I'm sure our presence is important. I plan to go there next."

"Good. Please ask for Gloria, the facility administrator. I told her you'd be coming."

"Thank you, Father Peter. Have a safe trip!"

The lobby of the Gilmore Adult Living Facility looked like a living room with couches, chairs, side tables, and lamps. The receptionist looked to be in her late sixties; she had gray hair and glasses. Beyond the receptionist desk were locked glass doors that could be opened only by the staff using the buttons on a wall panel.

"Hello. My name is Father Clearie. I'm here to see Gloria."

"Hello, Father Clearie. I'll let Gloria know you're here."

"Hello, I'm Gloria, the facility manager. Nice to meet you, Father Clearie."

"Gloria, Father Peter is leaving for a conference outside the country and asked that I visit with the residents here and talk to them spiritually."

"Yes, Father. That will be good. What days will you be visiting?"

"I thought Wednesdays and Saturdays."

"Okay. We'll look forward to having you here, Father."

"Thank you. Nice meeting you."

"Special Agent Roth, this is Special Agent Mulligan. I've arrived, and I met Father Peter, who's going to a conference and some vacation in Italy. In his absence, I've arranged to visit the facility two days a week."

"Special Agent Mulligan, you've made significant progress. I'm impressed. Please keep me posted. Let me know when you have some credible information about the Cosco family," said Special Agent Roth.

"Good morning, Father Clearie. It's good to see you here today," the receptionist said.

"Thank you for your welcome. I'm going to the chapel and visit for a while."

"Hello. Don't let me disturb your prayer," said Special Agent Mulligan.

"Hello, Father Clearie. I'm glad you're here. I wanted to talk to you about flowers," said a resident.

"Did you say flowers?"

"Yes. Please don't forget to water them, especially the pink tulips."

"I'll make sure not to forget. You have a nice day."

Just as I was reading some scripture, I heard a commotion in the hallway.

"Please come quick! It's Carlo! He's acting strange. The nurse is unable to give him his medicine," said a caregiver.

I watched as the caregivers rushed to room 108. I heard yelling.

"I don't want any pills," said Carlo.

"Carlo, you have to take these pills at ten every morning. Please stop giving Nurse Erin a hard time," said the caregiver.

"Thank you for helping me," said Nurse Erin.

Finally, I heard quiet in the area and assumed that the nurse had given him the pills. I decided to walk around the facility and began walking down the hallway toward Carlo's room.

"Excuse me," said Carlo.

"Are you talking to me?" Special Agent Mulligan asked.

"Yes I am."

"How can I help you?"

"Can you pray for me?"

"Why do you need prayer?"

"I need prayers for my family. They haven't visited me in a while. I want to see them."

"Sure. Dear heavenly Father, we pray that you will direct Carlo's family to come visit him soon, in Jesus's name, amen."

"Thank you, Father."

I visited the facility again on Saturday. I went into the small chapel with four pews and a gold-plated cross on the wall.

"Hello, Father Clearie," said Carlo.

"Hello, Carlo. How are you today?"

"I feel much better since the last time you saw me."

"Yes, you look better too. Have you heard from your family?"

"Yes, and they're coming to visit next Wednesday. I guess God heard your prayer."

"Who will be visiting you?"

"My dad, Tony, and my brother, Jacob."

"What about your mom?"

"My mom is deceased."

"I'm sorry."

"When she died, my father decided to bring me here."

"It was your father who decided you should be here?"

"He and my doctor."

"Who's your doctor?"

"Dr. Payne. He's a psychiatrist."

"Your family travels far to visit you."

"Yes. But my dad has a lot of business all around the country, and I have relatives in town."

"Do those relatives visit you?"

"Yes. Usually, when my dad and brother can't visit me, they come by to check on me. Father Clearie, I'm going to go back to my room."

"Okay, Carlo. I'll see you next week."

"Goodbye, Father Clearie."

The day was Wednesday. Carlo's father and brother were going to visit him.

"Do you know Dr. Payne?" Special Agent Mulligan asked a medications aide.

"Dr. Payne? No, that name isn't familiar. Why do you ask?"

"He's the doctor who comes here to visit with the residents. I'd like to speak with him. If you should come across this Dr. Payne, will you please let me know?"

"Yes I will, Father."

I walked past Carlo's room and heard voices. I walked to the chapel and sat. I got up to go to the water fountain, and Carlo's room door opened. Out walked his brother and father.

"Excuse me, but are you Carlo's family?" Special Agent Mulligan asked.

"Yes. Who are you?" asked Carlo's father.

"I'm Father Clearie. I visit with the residents here."

"Nice to meet you. Carlo never mentioned you," said Carlo's father.

"Nice to meet the both of you. I'm glad you came to visit Carlo. Where's home for you?"

"Canada. Have a nice day," said Carlo's father.

"Father Clearie, Carlo's asking to see you," said a caregiver.

"Is he coming to the chapel?"

"No. He asks that you go to his room."

"Carlo, it's Father Clearie."

"Hi, Father. Thanks for coming."

"I met your family."

"My father and brother?"

"Yes, and you resemble your brother."

"Father, I don't know, but I feel my family isn't honest."

"What do you mean?"

"I mean, when they visit me, it's only for about thirty minutes, and they leave. Sometimes, it's months between their visits, and all they can give me is thirty minutes?"

"Are you angry about that?"

"Yes I am. They always bring me things when they come to visit such as white chocolate. I don't understand why because I don't like white chocolate."

"Do they know you don't like white chocolate?"

"Yes, they know. I don't know why, but my brother Jacob puts the chocolate in the drawer and then takes the old chocolate I didn't eat from the last visit."

"What does Jacob do with the old chocolate?"

"Don't know. I think he puts it in the garbage."

"In your garbage?"

"No. He takes the chocolate with him."

"Carlo, I'll let you get some rest. I'll visit you again on Saturday."

"Hello, Special Agent Roth."

"Hello, Special Agent Mulligan."

"I wanted to update you. I've met several times with Carlo. I met his father and brother last Saturday. The next visit is coming up—Father's Day. Carlo expects them to come. Most important, he told me his brother always brings him a box of white chocolates, which he doesn't like. I think diamonds that were smuggled into the States are kept in the boxes of chocolates. It's obvious that his relatives who live here in Arizona are the ones who place the diamonds in the candy box for his father and brother to pick up when they come to visit. If you want to catch the Cosco family in the act, it would be on Father's Day."

"Excellent work. I do believe that's where the diamonds are kept. Don't be surprised if you get a visit from some FBI agents on Father' Day, Agent Mulligan."

It was Father's Day. The unexpected was about to happen at the facility.

"Tony and Jacob Cosco, you have the right to remain silent. Anything you say can and will be used against you in a court of law. You have the right to an attorney. If you cannot afford an attorney, one will be provided for you. Do you understand these rights?" the police officer asked.

"Yes," said Tony and Jacob.

The police car pulled off, and I left the facility before Carlo could see me or any of the FBI special agents could notice me. Operation Clearie was officially over.

Chapter 23

FATHER DILLION

"SPECIAL AGENT MULLIGAN, the FBI is very impressed with the work you conducted as an undercover priest in Tucson. You handled your assignment carefully, and your efforts were instrumental in helping us arrest Tony and Jacob Cosco," said Special Agent Roth.

"Thank you, sir. You were right when you told me this assignment would be a challenge."

"Arresting the Coscos was like discovering a gold mine. He's willing to cooperate with the FBI and has provided us with significant information that will allow us to begin phase two of this operation," said Special Agent Roth.

"Phase two?"

"Yes. I wanted to meet with you today to discuss your next undercover assignment. I do hope you kept your collar and robe."

"Yes I did."

"In your next assignment, which is still part of Operation Robe, you'll be involved in an FBI undercover operation on the international playing ground. We'll need you to go to Africa for six months as an undercover priest. We're sending you to a place called Orapa, in Botswana."

"Does the FBI have jurisdiction in Africa?"

"The FBI has jurisdiction anywhere on US soil. In a foreign country, the FBI can assist the local police with an arrest of someone wanted by the FBI, but the local police will have to make the arrest first. FBI agents have no law enforcement authority off U.S. soil.

"We have credible information that the person who got those diamonds to Tony Cosco lives in Africa. The FBI along with the government in

Botswana needs to capture the second target in this case, Abimbola Ballo. Once he's arrested, the FBI will use him to help us arrest those who helped him smuggle the diamonds into the United States."

"I didn't know there were more targets of this operation."

"There are. Let me tell you about the diamond mining business in Africa. First, forty-nine percent of diamonds originate from Central and Southern Africa. The assignment won't be difficult for you. Ballo is a devout Catholic. He's a member of a family that owns and operates one of the largest diamond mines in southern Africa."

"Are you referring to blood diamonds?" I asked.

"No. Blood diamonds are mined in war-zone countries, and Botswana isn't a war zone. However, this operation involves smuggling diamonds across African borders. We need to get the person who smuggled diamonds into the States."

"What will be my undercover name?"

"Father Dillion."

"Dillion? I see you're keeping me Irish."

"Yes I am, but Africa has a large Catholic population, so priests are very common on that continent, so you'll fit right in. Special Agent Walker, who works at the CIA in Botswana, will meet you at the airport. We need you to leave in two days. Special Agent Mulligan, you know the procedure when you're on assignment. I need you to be extremely careful since you won't be on American soil."

"Yes sir, I understand."

"You'll need to learn Tswana."

"Tswana?"

"Setswana is the national language in Botswana, but Tswana is the language spoken in Orapa, where you'll be living. The good news is that the natives in Orapa speak English, but we think it's important for you to learn the language. We have someone who works closely with the FBI and trains our agents. He has a method that he uses, and so far, our agents have learned many languages quickly."

"I'm looking forward to learning a new language, sir."

"It'll take three weeks for you to be fluent enough to speak and understand the language. Once you've learned it, you'll fly to Botswana and meet Special Agent Walker. He'll fill you in."

Chapter 24

BOTSWANA, AFRICA

"WELCOME, LADIES AND gentlemen to Gaborone in Botswana," the flight attendant announced.

"Hello, Special Agent Mulligan. I'm Special Agent Walker. I'll take you to where you'll be staying."

"Thank you. It's a pleasure to meet a US citizen."

"I'll take you first to CIA headquarters so I can explain to you the details of your stay here in Orapa. Follow me through security. I'm sure you know the drill."

"I'm glad you're here. We need your help, Special Agent Mulligan. I know Roth gave you some of the details of your assignment. I'll explain the geographical part of your assignment. The target of this operation is Abimbola Ballo. His family owns a diamond mine here in Orapa. It's the resting place for lions and the largest diamond mine in the world. We believe that the diamond mine is owned by the Ballos. The FBI is sure a member of the family was the distributor for Tony and Jacob Cosco," said Special Agent Walker.

"How does the FBI think I can help to catch Abimbola?"

"All in the Ballo family are devout Catholics. Several of the family attend Saint Christopher Catholic Church here in Orapa. However, one family member has been a frequent visitor to Father Carney, the priest at the church. We also know that he's involved in his family's illegal diamond mine business. The time couldn't be better for you to come to Botswana. Father Carney's going on a leave of absence for six months for personal reasons. We hope you'll be able to complete this assignment during his absence. I'll take you to the church where you'll reside until the assignment is completed," said Special Agent Walker.

Like many places in Africa, Botswana offers safaris and other wildlife attractions for tourists. Many pictures of animals such as zebras dominate the large billboards in town, and there are many restaurants there as well.

"Hello, and welcome to our restaurant. I see you're a foreigner," the waitress said.

"Yes I am, and this is my first time eating African food," said Special Agent Mulligan.

"My name is Susanna. I'll be your waitress. I can tell you that our most popular dish is called *seswaa*, our meat stew served over thick polenta or pap. The stew is made by boiling meat with onion and pepper. We serve this dish with our vegetable called *morogo*."

"Susanna, if you recommend it, that's what I'll order. May I have bottled water?"

"Here's your bottled water. May I ask what brings you to Botswana?"

"I'm here to fill in for Father Carney, the priest at Saint Christopher's."

"Father Carney? He's our priest!"

"You're a member of the church, Susanna?"

"Yes, for a long time. What's your name?"

"Father Dillion."

"Father Dillion. I see why you are filling in for Father Carney. He ate lunch here all the time, and his favorite dish is seswaa. You'll enjoy it, Father Dillion."

"Susanna, the food was delicious. I'm so glad you recommended it."

"Father Dillion, would you like some dessert and coffee?" asked Susanna.

"No. Next time. I really like the cream-colored décor with the masks and baskets on the walls. I'm ready for the check, please."

"Here's your check. I'll see you at Mass, Father Dillion."

"I look forward to seeing you at church, and I like your braids—very exotic looking on you."

"Thank you, Father."

Chapter 25

St. Christopher Catholic Church

I STOPPED BY THE CIA to visit with Special Agent Walker.

"Special Agent Mulligan, how are things progressing with Operation Father Dillion?" asked Special Agent Walker.

"I'm settled in here at the church. I've met the staff and have begun my assignment."

"Good. Thanks for letting me know."

So there I was at the church waiting for the day to begin, and in walks a dark-skinned, young woman wearing an African-print dress and sandals.

"Can I help you? My name is Father Dillion. I'll be filling in for Father Carney, who's on a leave of absence."

"Hello, Father Dillion. My name is Amiri. It's unfortunate we meet under these circumstances."

"What do you mean?"

"I'm here, Father Dillion, because my brother, Kwasi, was an African diplomat who traveled the world. He was recently killed in the Congo during a cultural war fight. His body is being flown back to Botswana so we can give him a proper burial. I am here to ask that you conduct his funeral."

"My condolences on the loss of your brother. I will say a special prayer for your family and ask God to comfort all of you."

"We'll have his body brought to the funeral home and then here to the church. Here's the information you will need about my brother."

"Amiri, I'll give this information to Enoila, our church secretary, so she can prepare and print the service program."

"Father Dillion, our family has a request for the funeral—someone to sing 'Ave Maria' by Franz Schubert."

"Yes, of course, Amiri. I will ask one of our choir members to do that."

"Thank you, Father Dillion. My family appreciates your spiritual kindness during our time of grieving."

"Good morning, Father Dillion. I've finished the program for Amiri's brother. The funeral home will deliver Kwasi's body here to the church this morning. I expect that some of the family will come by the church today," said Enoila.

"Thank you, Enoila. I'll be in the rectory if you need me," said Special Agent Mulligan.

"Hello, Special Agent Mulligan. You've been trying to reach me?" asked Special Agent Walker.

"Yes. I have a problem. A member of the church has died, and his family is having his funeral here at the church. I'll have to conduct his funeral."

"Don't worry. We'll make sure you have everything you need for that."

The church was filled with family and friends in black. Several stands of flowers were delivered to the church for Kwasi's family, and all the necessary candles and ceremonial items were in place.

"Father Dillion, everything is in place for the service," said Enoila.

"Thank you. I'm going to the coffin before they bring it inside," he replied.

I walked inside and saw a nun kneeling and praying over Kwasi's coffin. When I approached the coffin, she turned around. I was surprised to see Lindy from the FBI Academy.

"Father Dillion, good to see you. We don't have time to talk. I'm here to give you this earpiece. You'll receive instructions on how to conduct the funeral. Just listen and do as you're told. No time for questions. I must go. We'll see each other again. My name is Sister Catherine," said Special Agent McKnight.

"Family and friends, this concludes our Mass at Saint Christopher Catholic Church. We will proceed to the cemetery," said Special Agent Mulligan.

The day ended, and in walked Special Agent McKnight.

"I didn't know you'd be working on this assignment, Lindy."

"Remember, Special Agent Mulligan, when we graduated from the FBI Academy, I went to work overseas, and I've been to several countries. Now it's Botswana!"

"I'm glad you're here. It's good to see a familiar face. How long will you be here?"

"Until my assignment's complete."

"I didn't really think I would see you again, especially as a nun, Lindy."

"Does 'Until we meet again' sound familiar? If you're free later, let's meet for dinner at the Italian restaurant downtown."

"I had enough Italian back home. I know a good restaurant I think you'd like."

"Okay, I'll give it a try. I'll meet you at seven."

"Excuse me, Father Dillion, but what time does confession begin today?" a church member asked.

"At three. It goes until six."

"Thank you," said the church member.

"Forgive me, Father, for I have sinned. Father Dillion, my name is Abimbola. I heard that Father Carney is on a leave of absence."

"Yes, that's correct."

"I'm glad you're here. I got nervous when I learned about his absence."

"It sounds to me, Abimbola, that you come frequently to confession."

"I come every week. It's important for me to come."

"What sin would you like to confess today?"

"Father Dillion, I have many sins, but the one that concerns me the most is that I am very rich. My parents named me Abimbola, which means 'born be rich.'"

As Abimbola began talking, I turned on a tape recorder I had under my robe.

"Father Dillion, my family owns one of the largest diamond mines here in Orapa. Our family distributes diamonds to jewelers. However, I am involved in selling diamonds to those who put them on the black market. I can make triple the price set by our government," said Abimbola.

"Do you plan to stop selling diamonds illegally?"

"Stop? No, Father Dillion. That's how I became so rich."

"What do you want God to do for you if you still plan to engage in sin?"

"I would like God to know that I don't like to sell diamonds on the black market. But I feel that this is the only way I can get the true value of the diamonds. To be forgiven for my sins, I donate a lot of money to the church."

"How much?"

"Let's just say a large amount."

I heard the button on the tape recorder click. I realized I could no longer continue our conversation, so I let him know I would pray for his sins. I walked outside the confession booth and noticed that the church was empty. It was late, so I called it quits for the evening. I went back to the rectory to change my clothes and left to meet Special Agent McKnight for dinner.

"Father Dillion, it's nice to see you," said Special Agent McKnight.

"Yes, it's good to see you too, Sister Catherine."

"Welcome, Father Dillion. It's good to see you again," said Susanna.

"Thank you. This is Sister Catherine, Susanna."

"Please have a seat. What can I get you to drink?" asked Susanna.

"Bottled water will be fine for the both of us," he answered.

"What dish do you eat here?" asked Special Agent McKnight.

"Seswaa. It's stewed meat and vegetables."

"Sounds good."

"After dinner, I'll show you around downtown Orapa."

"I'd like to it. Thanks!" she said.

The week went well. Nothing unexpected happened. I thought Abimbola would come to confession. One by one, church members came to the confessional. Finally, I heard a voice I knew was Abimbola's. I turned on my tape recorder.

"Forgive me, Father, for I have sinned."

"Abimbola, what would you like to confess today?"

"I have come to confess that because of my evil ways of conducting business, I have caused friction in my family. Some people in other countries have spread the word to some leaders in Botswana that our family business is dealing in the black market."

"Who is saying this about your family?"

"People in Europe and the United States. They are people I decided not to do business with because someone offered me a better price for the diamonds. I have been told that my decision has angered some of these people, and I believe this is their way of getting back at me."

"Why are they spreading these rumors about your family if you are the only family member who is selling diamonds on the black market?"

"I don't know."

"What do you plan to do about the people who are spreading these rumors?"

"I don't know because my family doesn't know I sell the diamonds in the black market. I wanted to come to confession today and ask God for the answer to my problem."

"Let us pray for God to give you the answer. It may take some time before God answers your prayer, however."

"Yes, Father Dillion. Thank you for praying with me."

"Abimbola, I will see you next week at confession."

"Hello, Special Agent Mulligan. How's your assignment going?" asked Special Agent Roth.

"I'm glad you called. I was going to send you an email about my assignment. I have some good news about the target. Ballo has come to confession twice, and I've learned a lot about his family's diamond business. If he continues to come to confession weekly, I believe I could complete this assignment sooner than expected."

"I'm glad you're making progress. Please keep me posted," said Special Agent Roth.

"I will."

"I hope Special Agent Walker has been helpful to you."

"He has, and so has Special Agent McKnight."

"Father Dillion, I'm leaving early today. I have a parent-teacher conference at my daughter's school," said Enoila.

"I'll pray that the conference meets all your expectations about your daughter."

The day wasn't like an ordinary Wednesday when many church members would gather for confession. But as usual, the last church member was Abimbola.

"Forgive me, Father, for I have sinned," said Abimbola.

"What brings you to confession today?"

"There's been some feuding going on my family. It seems they're beginning to turn against me. At first, they didn't believe the rumors about our diamond business, but lately, their attitude has changed. My oldest brother, Ofie, wants to vote me out of the family business. He feels I have given the Ballo family a bad name."

"What will you do, Abimbola?"

"I'll finish doing business with three of my clients who are purchasing diamonds from me and then leave the family business. I have enough money to start my own business. One of my clients is coming to Botswana to purchase his diamonds. The other client I'm going to meet lives in Switzerland, and the third client lives in the United States."

"I think you should decide if you want to go through with these transactions."

"Oh, it's too late. Once a commitment is made, it's important to follow through. I can't back out of these business deals," said Abimbola.

"Let us pray that you will seek guidance on how to handle the difficult situation you are experiencing with your family."

Chapter 26

Change in Operation Robe

ONE DAY, I stopped by the Central Intelligence Agency to visit with Special Agent Walker. It was time to give him the report I had prepared regarding the target of this operation, Abimbola Ballo.

"Special Agent Mulligan, how are things progressing with Operation Father Dillion?" asked Special Agent Walker.

"The reason why I wanted to meet with you today is because I have gathered enough information from Abimbola Ballo and have prepared a report to conclude the assignment regarding my responsibility."

"I'm glad to hear that."

"He confessed information to me about his business dealings. First, he sells diamonds on the black market because he doesn't want to pay the duty tax required by the Botswana government."

"This is very important information. If Abimbola has admitted that he doesn't pay duty tax on the diamonds he exports, that will help our case. We'll request duty tax records from the government for Abimbola Ballo."

"At the last confession, he told me that there was friction in his family. Rumors have been spread that the diamonds have been sold illegally. It caused a feud between him and some of his siblings. He has three more business transactions in Botswana, Switzerland, and the United States. Once he's completed those business transactions, he plans to leave the family business."

"Did he indicate if he plans to leave the family business and relocate or start another business?"

"He told me he has enough money to start his own business. He will not be coming to confession this week because he plans to handle his business transactions. The first one is here in Botswana."

"You're sure he plans to sell diamonds to someone coming to Botswana?"

"Yes, and I assume it's going to be on Wednesday because he mentioned he wouldn't be coming to confession that day."

"This will help us arrest him. Good work, Agent!"

"At this time, I feel I've gained enough trust and confidence about the target. Here's the tape recorder I kept under my robe to record his confessions."

"Special Agent Roth will be very happy to hear this. So what's next for you?"

"Since the assignment here is for six months and Father Carney will be returning to the church next week, I plan to do some touring in Botswana. As it is said, Orapa is considered the resting place for lions."

Chapter 27

Father Liam

"SPECIAL AGENT ROTH is ready to meet with you," said the receptionist.

"Special Agent Mulligan, please come in," Special Agent Roth said. "I've been waiting to see you. I would like to commend you on your fine job with Operation Robe. The information you gathered for the FBI was incredible. I'm very impressed with your skills.

"Abimbola Ballo met with his client at a hotel in downtown Orapa. FBI agents learned that he rented a suite at a hotel and arranged to be in the room next to his suite. It was there that the FBI had an undercover maid place a listening device and a camera in the room. He met with his client and made the business transaction. His client gave him a suitcase filled with money," said Special Agent Roth.

"I'm glad the police arrested him."

"Special Agent Mulligan, I was so impressed with the way you handled your undercover assignment in Africa that I have one more assignment for you that will complete Operation Robe. The operation is here in the United States. We want to catch our target, Kane Bolin, who was the businessman smuggling diamonds into the United States. Bolin lives in New York and is one of Abimbola's clients. We need to capture him. With your help, we're confident we can do that."

"The Big Apple?"

"Yes. He lives in Manhattan, and he's a devout Catholic. The FBI has learned that he attends confession on Saturdays and Mass on Sundays. He owns a jewelry store in the diamond district. You'll be in contact with a special agent who will assist you just as Special Agent Walker did in Africa. Any questions?"

"Yes. What's my name for this undercover operation?"

"Father Liam. You'll live in an apartment in New York that's owned by the FBI. It's three blocks from the church where you'll be working, Our Lady of Lourdes, on 142nd Street in Manhattan. I must tell you that even though you'll be an undercover priest, it's important for you to know that New York is a big city in a small place. The Catholic religion is big in New York. There aren't numerous churches, and everyone knows each other. The reason I'm telling you this is because for this assignment, the FBI had to create a legitimate profile for you because in the priesthood, it's common for priests to research other priests," Special Agent Roth said.

"Your full name will be Liam Kennedy, and you will have studied theology at the Catholic Theological Union in Chicago, where you earned an MA in Catholic studies. There's a little history about the school you should know. It was founded in 1968 during a time of civil unrest in the United States prompted by the assassinations of Martin Luther King Jr. and John F. Kennedy as well as the Vietnam War.

"Father Michael, who is the priest at Our Lady of Lourdes, is from Chicago, and his favorite place to eat there is called Antique Taco on Milwaukee Avenue. The FBI wants you to know these facts in case he chooses to engage in conversation with you about Chicago. Father Michael is not at the church on Saturday, which is the day for confession. He teaches a religious course at the School of Divinity in Manhattan. Therefore, the church needs a priest who can be there from three to six in the afternoon on Saturdays to handle confessions."

"What course does Father Michael teach?"

"Intercultural religious studies at the School of Divinity. You'll be the acting priest in his absence for confessions only."

"When does this assignment begin?"

"Immediately. This operation is a little different because we've already captured Ballo. The only thing we need from the target of this operation is his admission that he smuggled diamonds into the United States."

"He only needs to admit his connection with Ballo in confession?"

"Yes. In New York, you'll meet with Special Agent Reilly. He'll give you additional details. Special Agent Mulligan, I'm very pleased you've accepted this assignment. It's very important to the FBI that we close this case."

"I understand. I look forward to the challenge."

"Good luck, Father Liam."

Chapter 28

Our Lady of Lourdes

"GOOD MORNING, FATHER Michael," said Special Agent Mulligan.

"Father Liam, you must have read my mind. I was just thinking about you. I'm glad to know you'll be handling confessions on Saturdays. Do you have any questions?"

"No questions, but I'd like a tour of the church. It always amazes me to see church architecture and design."

"Me too. It's amazing to see how Catholic churches around the world look. Here's the confession booth. Father Liam, I'm glad you came by. I look forward to seeing you on Saturday."

"Thanks for showing me the church. I'll come on Saturday."

"Hello, Donovan. I'm glad I was able to reach you," said Maureen.

"Hi, Mom! I'm glad to hear from you."

"Donovan, I have some bad news about Kenny. He got into some trouble and was arrested."

"Arrested?"

"Yes. Apparently, he came home and found his daughter, Adrienne, with a Hispanic guy she'd been dating whom he and Sherry hadn't known about. Kenny came home early from working at the firehouse because he wasn't feeling well and found the two of them in bed having sex."

"What?"

"Yes. And it gets worse. Kenny and the guy got into an argument, which led to a fight. Kenny stabbed the guy. He killed him, Donovan."

"Oh no! I can't believe this, Mom!"

"I wanted to tell you before you read about it in the papers or heard it from someone else."

"Where's Kenny now?"

"In jail. Uncle John will bail him out."

"I'm shocked!"

"I know you're busy, but when you get a chance, please call your cousin."

"I will. Tell Kenny to hang in there. Was it self-defense?"

"I don't know all the details, but it sounds like self-defense."

"Thanks for letting me know, Mom."

"Good afternoon. I'm Father Liam, and I'll hear confessions in Father Michael's place. Please step forward and enter the confession booth," I said.

I stepped outside the confession booth to use the bathroom and noticed a man fitting the description of the target of this operation, Kane Bolin.

"Father Liam, I read the sign at the entrance that you'll be conducting confessions," said Bolin.

"Yes, that's correct."

"Forgive me, Father, for I have sinned," said Kane.

"What would you like to confess today?"

"Father, I've been coming to confession for some time now, but now is more crucial than ever."

"Why's that?"

"I haven't been able to contact my business contact for the supplies I need to make jewelry."

"What kind of supplies?"

"Diamonds."

"Why have you been unable to contact your supplier?"

"I think he's gotten into trouble. Every time I called him, I went right to voice mail. Just today, I tried again, and his number wasn't in service. We had plans to make a business deal here in New York, but he never showed up."

"Who's your business contact?"

"His name is Abimbola Ballo. He lives in Botswana."

"Have you thought about going to Botswana to look for him?"

"No. I've never been to Africa. He always comes to New York with the diamonds."

"What are you confessing?"

"I'm confessing that I know he smuggled diamonds into the United States for me. I've been dealing with him for years, and it's not easy to find a new contact at his prices, if you know what I mean. My business will suffer greatly if I don't contact him soon."

"Let us pray that the Lord will bring Abimbola to you soon."

"Thank you, Father Liam, for the special prayer."

"Father Michael, I just finished my last confession. I was getting ready to go home."

"Father Liam, how was your first day of confession?" asked Father Michael.

"Good. Six people came."

"I'm glad everything went well. I'll see you at Mass tomorrow, Father Liam."

"Yes. I plan to attend the ten o'clock and the two o'clock masses."

I left the church and was hungry. Though I'd eaten before coming to the church, I felt like I needed a snack. I remembered seeing a diner across the street and went there.

"Here's your coffee and your grilled cheese," the waitress said.

"Special Agent Roth, it's Special Agent Mulligan."

"Special Agent Mulligan, how are things going with your assignment?"

"Things are going well. I met with Bolin at confession, and he shared a lot of information with me. I predict that after meeting with him two or more times, this assignment will be complete."

"Very good. I'm glad to hear that. Please keep me posted."

Once again, it was Saturday. I was going to handle confessions at Our Lady of Lourdes from three to six. Bolin was the first waiting for confession.

"Hello, Kane. Nice to see you," I said.

"Father Liam, I'm glad you're having confession today. I have a lot to confess before I go to Africa."

"Please step inside the confession booth."

"Forgive me, Father, for I have sinned."

"What would you like to confess today?"

"Father Liam, I'd like to confess that I am still trying to communicate with my business contact, Abimbola, who smuggles the diamonds into the United States that I buy."

"What will you do about that?"

"I'm going to Africa and will try to find him."

"Are you sure that's what you want to do?"

"Father Liam, I won't come to confession next week because I'll just be returning from Africa, but I promise to come to confession the following week to continue our discussion."

A few more people came for confession. I went back to my apartment and emailed Special Agent Roth about the confession session with Kane. I put on some blue jeans and an Irish-green cardigan sweater and shirt. Since I knew I'd be doing a lot of walking, I put on my black loafers. I grabbed my backpack, which held a map of New York and a bottle of water. I started touring the city. I took the M4 bus uptown to 190th Street, and I walked to the Cloisters Museum at 40 Tryon Park in Washington Heights. After I toured the area, I took the subway downtown and saw *Jesus Christ Superstar* at the Center for the Performing Arts.

"Donovan Mulligan! I thought that was you. What are you doing in New York?" Special Agent Dominick asked.

"Dominick Porelli! I'm surprised to see you. I'm here on assignment. What about you? I see you're wearing your FBI jacket."

"After the academy, I came back to New York and got a job at FBI headquarters here. It's been nonstop since my first day," Special Agent Porelli said.

"I'm just checking out the city myself."

"I just had lunch with my wife, who works in the city too. I'm heading back to headquarters. Here's my number. Make sure to visit me before your assignment ends, Donovan."

"Yes, I will. And I saw Lindy when I was on assignment in Africa."

"How's she doing?"

"She's doing fine, but I haven't been in contact with her since I left Africa."

"Take care, Donovan."

"You too, Dominick."

"Hello, Special Agent Mulligan," said Special Agent Roth.

"Special Agent Roth, I was just typing my report on Bolin and was just about to hit the save button when you called."

"That's the reason for my call. The FBI learned from the US embassy in Botswana that Bolin's dead. He was making a call on his cell when an explosion went off just outside his hotel. He was standing right where the explosion occurred. Killed instantly, according to the report."

"That's a shock. He said he'd be back to New York to go to confession."

"Special Agent Mulligan, you've done a fine job so far. Any information you have will help us close this case."

"I'll finish my report and email it to you immediately. It's interesting that Bolin shared so much information with me about his business dealings involving diamonds. I guess this was how it was going to end for him."

"Yes. Send the report, and then take a vacation, Agent."

"I plan to visit family in Boston."

"We'll meet when you return."

"Thanks for letting me know the news about Bolin."

Chapter 29

Back in Boston

"GOOD MORNING, DONOVAN Michael Mulligan. When did you get home?" asked Mom.

"Last night. I just went to bed. I'm going to visit Kenny at the Kingston Correctional Facility."

"Good, Donovan. He'd like to see you. It's been a while. I'm sure he has a lot to tell you. Since he decided to take a plea bargain instead of going to trial, he should be out of prison soon."

"And I'll visit Father Carmichael too."

"Oh, Donovan. I thought you knew he retired. He's living in a retired priests' home in Upstate New York."

"Do you know where?"

"No, but I'm sure someone at the church can tell you."

"Father Carmichael finally had enough of the Mulligans!"

It had been a long time since I'd last visited St. Cardinal's. It seemed strange without Father Carmichael there.

"Excuse me, do you know where the church secretary is?" I asked.

"Yes, she's downstairs. Can I help you with something? I'm Father McGuiness."

"I was a member of this church. I heard that Father Carmichael retired."

"That's true. He's at a retirement home in Upstate New York."

"Do you have his address?"

"No, but if you give me your information, I can get it to him."

"Thanks. Here's my phone number and email address."

"I'll make sure he gets your message, Donovan," said Father McGuiness.

"Hey, it's my favorite nephew. Where are you?" asked Uncle John.

"I driving to Kingston to visit Kenny," I said.

"Oh, I'm glad to hear that. He'll be happy to see you. It's been so hard, Donovan, for Kenny being away from his family."

"I know, Uncle John. I kept Kenny in my prayers."

"Are you home for good now?" asked Uncle John.

"Until my next assignment."

"Have you talked to Patrick?"

"No, but I plan to visit with him when I return from visiting his father. I'll come and visit you too, Uncle John."

"I look forward to seeing you, Donovan. Give my son a big hug for me."

"I will. Goodbye, Uncle John."

The correctional facility in Kingston, New York, was on a piece of property with hundreds of acres and woods. It looked like a typical state prison with lots of barbwire surrounding most of the facility. There were very few windows in the brick buildings.

"Please put all of your personal items including your watch and shoes on the conveyor belt. Now, walk through the security check," said the security guard.

"I'm here to see Kenny Mulligan," said Donovan.

"Yes, Mr. Mulligan. He'll be notified that he has a visitor. Please sign the visitor log. You can go in the waiting area until the correctional officers bring him down to the visiting area."

"Thank you."

I walked in the waiting room, where others were waiting. I didn't know how long it would be until they brought Kenny down. About an hour later, I heard my name called.

"Donovan Mulligan?" asked a security guard.

"Yes?"

"Please follow me."

"I can't believe my eyes! Is that my cousin Donovan?" Kenny asked.

"Hey, Kenny! Long time, huh?"

"Yes. It's great to see you, Donovan. I thought you were my lawyer. This is truly a surprise."

"I just came home from my last FBI assignment and wanted to visit my cousin."

"I'm glad you did. I have a lot to tell you, Donovan. Where should I begin?"

"Tell me about the situation here in prison."

"The two guys who were responsible for your father's murder are here. Santiago, the trigger man, found out I was your father's nephew, and all hell brook loose. He began to spread the word that I was the nephew of a cop just to stir up trouble.

"One day, he and I were assigned to clean the machinery room, and we fought. While we were fighting, we banged into a piece of machinery. He fell, and it sliced his ear in half. He screamed, and blood started to pour out of his ear. The correctional officers came running and took him to the prison clinic. He had to be rushed to the hospital for surgery. The warden here decided he was a threat to the prison and had him transferred. I was reprimanded for my actions."

"Kenny, the last thing I wanted to hear from you was that you were in a fight with one of the guys responsible for killing my dad."

"I wanted that thug to know there were consequences for messing with a Mulligan. Donovan, I want you to be there for my son, Patrick."

"Sure, Kenny. I'm his godfather. I'll make sure he always stays on the right path."

"You sound like Father Carmichael. Speaking of Father Carmichael, did you know he retired?"

"Yes. I'm going to visit him."

"How's Lauren doing?"

"She's fine. She's raising Sandeen."

"Sandeen?" asked Kenny.

"Yes, she's your first cousin."

"She has a daughter?"

"Yes. That's a story. Sailors come to Maryland during summer. Lauren was invited to a party and met someone named Philip. Let's just say she had a fun time one night."

"Oh wow. So where's Philip?"

"In the navy. He sends Lauren money to help take care of Sandeen. I haven't met her yet, but I will when she comes to Boston to visit my dad's grave. How's Sherry handling your situation?"

"Donovan, she's handling it as best she can. She's always been a good wife. I can't tell you the sacrifices she's made. I know it's been hard financially."

"When was the last time she came here?"

"Over Christmas, but once the winter weather started, she stopped coming. I expect to see her soon. You should visit her. I know she'd be happy to see you, Donovan."

"I will when I return to Boston."

"Excuse me, Mr. Mulligan, but your time's up for visiting," said a security guard.

"Yes, I know … just one more minute. Kenny, anything you need?"

"Just your prayers, cousin. Your support and visit today is greatly appreciated and makes me feel there's hope. Please give hugs to all my family members when you see them."

"I will. Take care, Kenny."

I drove to Father Carmichael's retirement community. It was a big place with plenty of windows. I entered the place and signed the guest log. A young woman with blond hair wearing a blue blouse met me.

"Hello," said the receptionist.

"Hello. I'm here to see Father Carmichael."

"Just walk down the hall and turn right. He's the first door with a cross on it."

"Father Carmichael, it's been a long time. Now that my assignment with the FBI is completed, I wanted to come and talk with you."

"Donovan, I'm so glad you came. It makes me proud to know that you're one of the young men from church who'd come and visit with me."

"I just saw Kenny."

"I pray all the time that God will guide him, Donovan."

"He accepted a plea deal, so he should be getting out of prison soon."

"I'm glad to hear that."

"Father, so much has happened over the years that I don't know where to begin."

"Donovan, is this going to be a confession?"

"I don't know, Father."

"The reason I'm asking is that if you'd like to confess any sins, we'd need to do it in a church."

"Father, I just wanted to come and see how you were doing."

"I retired when I began to show signs of arthritis. I gave the archdiocese time to find someone to take my place at church."

"I can understand your decision to retire. The church has lost a special spiritual leader."

"Thank you, Donovan. Tell me what your plan is now that you're back home in Boston."

"I plan to keep working for the FBI, but there are some things I'd like to do before I go back to work."

"Were you able to seek out Catholic churches during your travels?"

"Yes, I did—several. I'm glad to see you're doing well and enjoying retirement, Father. I promise I'll come and visit with you again."

"Good to see you, Donovan. I'll continue to pray for you as you embark on a new journey with the FBI."

"Thank you, Father."

Chapter 30

END OF OPERATION ROBE

"GOOD MORNING, SPECIAL Agent Roth," said Special Agent Mulligan.

"Today is the day Special Agent Mulligan will be released from Operation Robe," said Special Agent Roth.

"We've heard nothing but good things about how you handled this undercover operation from the beginning, Special Agent Mulligan," said Special Agent Johnson.

"Thank you. I'm happy it was successful," said Special Agent Mulligan.

"I must say that you wore the priest collar well. The way you helped the FBI capture Ballo was crucial to our operation," said Special Agent Roth.

"He wasn't an easy target. It took me time to gain his confidence, but once I did, he confessed."

"The unfortunate situation with Bolin has brought Operation Robe to an end, but I must say that the information you got from him was very helpful," said Special Agent Roth.

"Yes, it was unfortunate that he was killed in Africa. I guess the saying that all good things come to an end was meant for Bolin," said Special Agent Mulligan.

"Special Agent Mulligan, what was the most challenging part of this operation for you?" asked Special Agent Roth.

"The most challenging part of the operation was the fact that I'm a devout Catholic and believe in confession. I never thought the day would come when I'd have to hear confessions. There's a lesson to be learned—be careful to whom you say, 'Forgive me, Father, for I have sinned.' Criminals don't realize that God doesn't honor those who want to hurt or kill others."

"The FBI trained you to use the tools necessary to help capture some of the world's most-wanted criminals. Special Agent Mulligan, a job well done! What's next for you?" asked Special Agent Roth.

"I plan to see if there are any FBI positions in Boston."

"Special Agent Mulligan, I came to this meeting to welcome you to the Medal of Honor club. Yes; because of your brave and courageous acts during this undercover operation, the FBI will be awarding you the FBI Shield of Bravery medal," said Special Agent Johnson.

"Congratulations, Special Agent Mulligan. And don't worry about Boston. I'll call my associate there and arrange for you to meet with him," said Special Agent Roth.

"Thank you very much!"

"Please keep in touch, Special Agent Mulligan. Maybe one day, I'll visit Boston with my family and go to a Red Sox game," said Special Agent Roth.

After Operation Robe ended, I boarded a plane for Boston. The flight attendant was gracious and gave me a pillow. I stared at the clouds and finally fell asleep. I began to dream.

"Hi, son," Donovan heard someone say. It sounded like his father.

"Dad, is that really you?"

"Yes, son, it is. I thought it was time that I came to visit you. I have been with you during your FBI assignments. I'm so proud of you, son. I'm most proud to know that you let your anger go about what happened to me."

"You knew I was angry?"

"Yes, and I'm glad you consulted with Father Carmichael for spiritual guidance. He's a good man and a good spiritual guide. Donovan, I'm always with you in spirit. The reason I picked this trip to visit with you is because there's a surprise waiting for you in Boston."

At that point, I woke up. I couldn't determine whether I'd been dreaming or if seeing and talking to my father had been real. I went to the washroom to wash my face and took a deep breath. I walked back to my seat. The pilot announced that we'd be landing in twenty minutes.

The plane finally landed. I was back home in Boston. What was different about that plane ride was that I had to go through a special gate for FBI clearance—the same gate celebrities use at the airport. All my items were searched, and my ID was cleared.

I began walking and dropped my cell phone. I turned around when I heard someone ask, "Excuse me, sir, but is this your phone?" I looked up and couldn't believe my eyes. Prince was handing me my phone. I told him that he'd been my favorite pop star when I was growing up and that I used to get good grades in school just so my dad would take me to see him in concert.

I told him about seeing him in concert on March 28, 1985, at the Centrum, a day I'd never forget for two reasons—it was the best concert ever, and it was the day my father was killed. Prince looked stunned. "May I have your autograph?" I asked him. "Yes," he said. He signed my handkerchief, which happened to be purple. He acknowledged me as a fan and quietly kept walking.

As I walked to my car, I thought about the two mysterious things that had happened to me that day—my dad visiting me in a dream, and seeing and even talking to Prince at the airport. I guessed that was what my dad meant when he said I had a surprise coming in Boston. I started my car and turned on the radio. I heard "Let's Go Crazy" by Prince.

"Donovan, welcome home! How was your visit with Father Carmichael?" Mom asked.

"Father Carmichael's doing well. He has arthritis. That's why he said he retired. He was glad I came to visit him. He said to tell you hello."

"Good. I'm glad you visited him. And meet your niece, Sandeen. Sandeen, this is your Uncle Donovan," Mom said.

"I finally get to meet my little niece. Where's your mom?" I asked.

"Lauren went to get a manicure and pedicure. She should be back soon," Mom said.

"Sandeen, who's that you're carrying?" I asked.

"This is Sugar Bear. He goes everywhere I go."

"This is your buddy, huh? She looks just like Lauren. She's a little twin," I said.

"She doesn't just look like Lauren. She also looks like a Mulligan," Mom said.

"Yes, she does, and here's my sister!" I said.

"Hey Donovan, glad to see you. I can see you've met your niece," Lauren said.

"Yes I did, and Mom was just saying she looks like a Mulligan."

"Mom, what are the plans for Sunday?" Lauren asked.

"We'll visit Dad's grave, just the Mulligan side of the family."

On March 28, the Mulligan family visited my dad's grave. We stayed for about an hour, and then we saw a black car pull up. Kenny, Patrick, and Father Carmichael got out of the car. We couldn't believe it.

"Kenny, we're so glad to see you! Father Carmichael, you too," I said.

"I'm in Boston because St. Cardinal's is having an anniversary for priests who served at the church. I took this moment to catch up with the Mulligans and thought by chance all of you would be here. I see some new Mulligans," said Father Carmichael.

"Yes, Father. This is my daughter, Chancy, and sons, Matthew and Quinn," said Timothy.

"This is Sandeen, Lauren's daughter," Mom said.

"You were right. The Mulligan family has indeed expanded," said Father Carmichael.

"Father Carmichael, would you take a picture of us?" Mom asked.

"Sure."

My family stood on either side of Dad's gravestone. Father Carmichael counted to three, and we yelled, "Mulligan!"

About the Author

Renee Smith resides in Charlotte, North Carolina.

Read her other books, *Talking Hats*, a must-read children's book, and *Code Blue*, a must-read suspense novel.

Printed in the United States
By Bookmasters